THE BODY THEY MAY KILL

THE BODY THEY MAY KILL

AUDREY STALLSMITH

THOMAS NELSON PUBLISHERS
Nashville • Atlanta • London • Vancouver

Published in Nashville, Tennessee, by Thomas Nelson, Inc., Publishers, and distributed in Canada by Word Communications, Ltd., Richmond, British Columbia.

Scripture quotations are from the KING JAMES VERSION of the Bible.

Library of Congress Cataloging-in-Publication Data

Stallsmith, Audrey.
    The body they may kill / Audrey Stallsmith.
        p. cm.
    ISBN 0-7852-7713-7
    I. Title.
PS3569.T3216B63 1995
813'.54—dc20   94-47000
                                                     CIP

Printed in the United States of America

1 2 3 4 5 6 — 00 99 98 97 96 95

Let goods and kindred go,
This mortal life also;
The body they may kill;
God's truth abideth still.
His kingdom is forever.

MARTIN LUTHER:
A Mighty Fortress Is Our God

To my mom and dad
for all their love,
loans, and long-suffering.

**Wherefore whosoever shall eat
this bread, and drink this cup
of the Lord, unworthily, shall
be guilty of the body and
blood of the Lord.**
I Corinthians 11:27

Murder, Genna Leon thought, *should be the last thing on anyone's mind in a small country church on a bright Easter morning.*

From across the aisle, Meredith DeWitt glowered at the ornately ugly cross strung about Genna's neck. *She's wearing that awful piece of jewelry again.* Meredith had once pointed out to the other woman that the cross in question was not in the best of taste. To which Genna had murmured, "Well, I don't suppose the real one was either, do you?"

One would expect an artist to have more concern about her appearance—that dress, for instance. Genna made a lot of her own clothes. This fact was all too painfully obvious. They tended to sag and pucker in unexpected places, not to mention that the patterns must have been highly erratic to begin with. The artist freely admitted her own deficiencies as a seamstress. "I just like making things," she would explain breezily, "and this keeps my hands busy when I'm not painting. See this piece," she pointed out once. "It was actually supposed to go over here, but I do hate ripping seams." All this had been uttered with a perfectly straight face, but Meredith got the uncomfortable impression on that occasion that Genna found *her* amusing.

Meredith wrenched her repulsed gaze away from the necklace to focus on the well-bred lines of her own ensemble. Not as expensive as Leona Bentley's, of course, but she liked to think that she wore it better. Leona slouched; also, her face was haggard and badly made up. *Hungover again,* Meredith thought. *Poor Elliot. What an impossible family he has.* His daughter, Tanya, on his other side, was literally plastered with a shocking shade of eyeshadow that made her sullen eyes even darker.

Tanya caught Meredith's patronizing stare and stared back with deliberate insolence. *Miz Upwardly Mobile herself,* Tanya thought, *with her discreetly applied makeup, discreetly understated suit, and discreetly handsome husband.* Blond and in an expensive tan jacket that made mockery of all the farmers in their dark suits, Garth DeWitt was easily the best-looking man in the room—and the biggest bore. Not to mention his being an accountant, which made him, for Tanya, virtually nonexistent.

Her impatient gaze drifted on to one of the farmers, Adam Cullen. *A male version of Meredith. The upwardly mobile farmer.* He had moved here from the next county, bought a large farm, installed all the latest equipment. At thirty, he was doing better than others in their fifties and sixties. It had not made him popular.

"That's not farming," Ben Grover, one of the older men, had sneered. "That's running a milk factory."

Genna, too, had been difficult, muttering in a grim little voice something about animals wearing serial numbers like machines. *Poor Adam.* Tanya smirked reminiscently. Genna had been the glitch in his smoothly running operation from the time of her arrival—five years before—upon her inheritance of the small farm next door to his.

For one thing, he had planned on adding that place to his own extensive acreage after old man Leon passed on. But Leon, a pinched, miserly, and regressive sort hadn't liked Adam, and got his revenge by leaving the farm to his niece with the condition that not one of his acres ever be sold or leased to his neighbor.

To make matters worse, the niece had adopted a

virtual menagerie, including a cat, a goat, and a horse with the respective names Grimm, Gruff, and Gratis. As the name indicated, the horse had come to her free. Judging from the animals' personalities, people rather suspected that the other two had also.

The fences on old Leon's place had been in a state of disrepair. And, between her painting and putting in a "little garden," Genna hadn't got around to doing much about them. Thus the horse and goat had taken to roaming Adam Cullen's picture-perfect fields. Tanya had been reluctantly on hand—standing in for her mother at a meeting of the local garden club—one Saturday when Adam, sputtering furiously, came pulling the goat along on a rope lead.

He was right in the middle of a group of curious women before he fully realized that he had an audience. Then, with barely controlled venom, he asked Genna what she planned to do about her animals trampling his corn.

Genna had been giving a talk on using herbs in cooking and, a bowl on one arm, was looking vaguely around her for a spoon to stir its contents. She located the spoon before answering and vigorously agitated the mess in the bowl. Then her gaze traveled meaningfully from the six-foot-six brawny farmer down to her diminutive goat, that, head hanging, was looking especially pathetic. She pointed at Adam's Border collie and said, "It's because you *chase* her, you see. With you and that

4

animal after her, of course she gets terrified and crashes through things. Really, how much harm can my wee little goat do to your great big fields?"

Here she gestured vigorously with the spoon in the direction of the fields and succeeded in walloping him alongside the face with a gob of tarragon-laced dough.

The women of the garden club barely repressed snickers. When the goat made a movement and the much-hassled dog, thinking it was getting away again, lunged snapping at its heels, the audience became openly hostile. There were mutters of, "Big bully," and, "Who does he think he is anyway?"

The goat wisely kept its head down and continued to look persecuted. Genna added, "But of course I'll pay you for any damage," and looking even more than usual like the poor but persevering waif, went looking for her purse.

The temperature of the meeting dropped another few degrees, everyone knowing that Genna's inheritance had been meager at best, and that it was only sporadically supplemented by her art. Realizing that things were getting away from him, but not quite understanding why, Adam muttered, "Never mind," and went away. The dog, at least, had enough sense to put its tail between its legs. At the memory, Tanya was hard put to sustain her bored expression against an irresistible desire to giggle. She had had a new respect for Genna after that.

The local farmers couldn't get enough of this story. Even some who would have, without compunction, shot the animal if it had ventured into their fields were squarely on Genna's side. This, of course, really had little to do with Genna herself. The reverend had preached a sermon on jealousy shortly thereafter.

Oblivious of Tanya's attention, Adam was in a half-doze with his eyes open—his thoughts drifting and fragmentary. In the pew in front of him, Genna put a hand to her slipping hairdo, and Cullen's gaze automatically veered away. He had learned to ignore her and her wretched animals as much as possible.

He wondered vaguely why Max Rourke, who was an atheist, persisted in coming out to church. Rourke was their local celebrity. A writer of satirical novels, he had a habit of using thinly veiled portraits of his friends and neighbors as his characters—which explained why he was running a little short in the friends category. Cullen's gaze drifted on to the clock. In his scheme of things, Rourke was an irrelevancy.

Max would have been irritated by this attitude had he known about it. He was watching the pastor's cousin with a critical eye. A neat and dowdy little woman probably close to forty, she had turned up one Sunday morning in the second seat from the front and had occupied it ever since. Nobody knew much about her. Enoch had brought her back from somewhere to keep house for him. There were rumors about a domineering female relative who had kept Ellen in a state bordering on neuroticism until that relative's death. She was certainly withdrawn enough. But boring, Max decided.

The whole world lately was tinged with the gray of banality. He could even taste it in his food—a flat stale flavor. His way with words was failing him too. His publisher had returned his latest effort. It had been mostly about the Reverend Enoch Foster, the person who irritated him more than anyone else in this God-forsaken backwater. He thought he'd pretty well torn the man and his faith into bite-size pieces. But the editor had written, "What's wrong with you, Max? You getting religion or something? You're losing your edge."

A couple of the ushers were getting quietly out of their seats—*almost squeaking,* he thought disgustedly, *like serious and well-behaved tots in their shiny tight suits. The children will be having their crackers and juice anytime now.* He was all at once so irrationally, so violently angry that he almost wept tears of frustration and rage. He felt the pastor's gaze on him. *The old man wouldn't have minded the book anyhow; he would only have been amused.*

Ellen Foster listened intently to Enoch's words. It had been only lately that she had been able to concentrate on his sermons and not on the critical eyes she was sure must be boring into her back. People must surely think her a charity case. But there was nothing else she could do, nowhere else she could go. She wasn't even a good cook and housekeeper; her great-aunt had reminded her of that often enough. An obsessively religious woman of the scare-the-devil-out-of-them persuasion, that aunt had "taught humility" by telling a sensitive little girl constantly how sinful and lazily incompetent she was. It only needed a few graphic descriptions of "the place where bad girls go" to spur Ellen on to more frantic efforts, none of which seemed quite adequate. Ellen had been with that aunt for thirty years.

It had been a good thing that, when the woman died, Ellen's only other close relative, an uncle on furlough from his mission in Africa, had been available to handle things. By then Ellen was little more than a nervous shadow, incapable of any decisive action on her own. She hardly knew her uncle Frank; he had been stateside so seldom. She overheard part of a phone call he made after the funeral. "I should never have let that woman have her. I realize that now. But I didn't know what I would do with a child in Africa; now I see it would have been considerably less dangerous than what she went through here.

"But I have to get back there, Enoch. Things are heating up; it's going to be war any day now. Under those circumstances, I can't take her with me, and she certainly can't cope alone. Can you do anything?"

What Enoch Foster could—and would—do was to fly halfway across the country to take a woman he had never seen back home with him. It turned out that he was a relative too—of a distant sort. Their last names were the same at least.

Ellen's experience with ministers had been anything but good. When she was sixteen, one who was supposed to be counseling her had fondled her rather too closely. Her aunt refused to believe her, adding contradictorily that, even if it was so, she must have been behaving seductively. The man in question, a heavyweight pompous sort with flat, greasy hair, had given his solemn opinion that the girl was a "problem child" and commiserated with the aunt on the burden this must be to her.

Enoch Foster had turned out to be frail-looking and seventyish, but had an infectious enthusiasm. He had found his first plane trip "fascinating." Frank's phone call had been "absolutely providential." Because, as he explained, "I'm old and absentminded, my dear, and inclined to be messy, and they have been telling me that I must get someone to cook and clean, and here you are!"

By the time they got back to the rural community where he had lived for most of his ministry, he had Ellen almost believing that it was she who was doing him a favor. His home was Spartan in almost everything but books. Of those he had a lavish hoard that seemed to spread and multiply into every room.

She had set out to earn her board by a zealous house-cleaning and had been stopped almost at once. "Martha, Martha," he had teased her, "thou art careful and troubled about many things." He preferred his cheerful welter. "Otherwise," he explained, "I can never find anything."

So there was little left for her to do but cook and, through a long cold winter, read. There had been very few books that her aunt permitted. Enoch, it seemed, had everything in the religious line from Augustine to Billy Graham, and a few that were downright agnostic. "One has to keep track of the competition," he explained with a wink. Not to mention a colorful array of fiction, supplemented by his forays at rummage sales.

In books by the likes of C. S. Lewis and G. K. Chesterton, she discovered a God completely different than the one she'd heard so much about, a God to whom her cousin talked as naturally as he talked to her. This had completely unnerved her the first few times she heard him. He explained apologetically that he had got used to praying out loud from his many years of living alone and hoped it wouldn't bother her. It was not like any praying that she had ever encountered—more like conversation with an old but occasionally obdurate friend. Enoch would stomp and wave his arms about and occasionally pull at his hair. Sometimes he would rush to his desk in the study, leaf feverishly through a well-thumbed Bible and point to a verse. "There!" he would exclaim in triumph. "There!" Other times she would find him lying across that same desk, weeping silently—this usually after there had been some especially nasty crime reported in the newspaper or some member of his congregation was suffering. No wonder so many of them thought he needed looking after. He had what seemed an almost foolish lack of self-consciousness and felt both joy and sorrow with a childlike intensity.

Perhaps that was why he got along so well with children. Many times that winter, she heated cocoa inside, while outdoors Enoch and some of his young friends spread out maps and plotted battle strategy for very serious snowball wars, muttering about enemy offenses and defenses. She had even consented once to be the captive lady rescued by her gallant knights, and laughed as she had never laughed before.

Enoch's habit became contagious. She had only ever dared approach God on her knees after a requisite litany of self-reproaches and placations. But now she found herself addressing Him spontaneously, and her most frequent beginning these days was a fervent, "Thank you."

Now, she felt indeed a spring in her heart, a freshness like Genna's impudently careless arrangement of daffodils on the altar, a jubilance like the tulips that even Meredith's stiffer wiring couldn't restrain. The freshness of wide open spaces and immense possibilities.

Murder should be the last thing on anyone's mind. Or perhaps it should be the first.

Genna Leon's restless fingers moved from her hair to the cross around her neck. She was thinking of something that Dorothy Sayers had written once—to the effect that people horrified by a cat killing a bird could hear the story of the killing of God Sunday after Sunday without any shock at all. Murder that had been, certainly. Perpetuated by the "nice" people of a community who had hopes of hanging on to that label.

Sayers had written a few good civilized murders of her own. Looking vaguely up at the stained glass window behind the pastor's head, Genna thought, *But only in this premeditated homicide of a Galilean carpenter can the Author point the finger of guilt at the reader.*

On a corner table at the back of the sanctuary, the communion elements rested under white linen. Dusty wafers and lukewarm grape juice. The body and the blood. The reality of that suddenly striking her, Genna almost gagged. Look, it seemed to be saying, even of this crime, you will be forgiven. But not until you look in its face, recognize it, drink it down.

A gory religion, some called it. But then, God was always a realist.

She dragged her attention guiltily back to the pastor's face. He was a good man, old Enoch Foster. Willing to love the sinner, but never to compromise the truth. *Which might make him a very dangerous man too.*

Ellen watched solicitously as Enoch came to stand in front of the altar for the communion service. He'd had a touch of the flu this past week, which was why the Good Friday service had been canceled and why they were taking the bread and wine during the Easter celebration instead. Enoch had insisted that he was recovered. They'd risen early that morning for the community sunrise service. And although he agreed to cancel his adult Sunday school class, he spent the time usually dedicated to that over in the church anyhow—studying and praying about his sermon. So that now he looked pale and a little tired. But he was never the type to complain. Self-pity was, to him, linked to that most repulsive of sins—ingratitude.

The ushers began passing around salvers of tiny silver goblets, of crisp little wafers. "Take, eat; this is my body." It said more to Ellen. *There is plenty of what I Am. You can never get enough.*

"This is my blood of the new testament, which is shed for many for the remission of sins." The last goblet was passed to Enoch Foster. It was larger than the others, graven with a cross, a gift from his congregation. He lifted it to his lips; he and the congregation drank as one.

Ellen was smiling again as she lowered her own small cup, waited expectantly for him to go on. Sunlight blazed through the window over his head. When he staggered, gagged, put an almost apologetically inquiring hand to his throat, she waited for him to catch his balance. Then he began to fold, crumpling down and down into the rainbow-bright colors of the sunshine in front of the flowers, in front of the altar.

She looked at him with dull incomprehension. A harsh, strained kind of hush fell over the room. Then Adam Cullen jerked up from his seat on the far left side of the room, ran to the front, bent over the crumpled figure, and put a hand to the base of the throat. Then, with grim practicality, he turned the pastor's body over and began to administer CPR. He was a volunteer fireman. *One might have known*, Ellen thought vaguely, *that he'd be as good at it as he was at other things*. Genna Leon turned in a whirl of skirts and ran down the aisle towards the back.

Other men were moving forward now, with slow, compelled action. At least, it seemed slow to Ellen. She held onto the back of the pew in front of her so tightly that her nails dug into the varnish. Genna returned, a flash of color amidst the dark suits. "The ambulance is on the way," she said. "How is—"

Adam Cullen shook his head at her without looking up from his concentrated task. Genna stood there, hand curled around her cross, looking down at Enoch's peaceful face. Then her lifting gaze met Ellen's. Her own seemed to clear a bit. She came with brisk, purposeful steps to sit beside the other woman. She didn't try to touch, or offer comfort, and that was a relief. She just sat and watched the men working over the body and others milling helplessly about. Joe Lawson, Adam's hired man, stared at Ellen, his rather stupid face stretched into an excited grimace—almost like a grin. His hungry gaze slid on to other faces, drinking in their shock and consternation, almost as if, Ellen thought, he was starved for excitement, and even tragedy would do.

When the ambulance came, they tried to shock the frail body into life, and Ellen turned her face away. But Genna watched with strange impassiveness.

They continued the attempts to revive him as they took him away. "Well, I think we might as well go back to the house now," Genna said. The other women seemed relieved that she had taken over with Ellen. There were sympathetic murmurs and brief pats on the shoulder, and Ellen found herself somehow back in her own kitchen which smelled of the Easter ham slow-cooking in the oven. Now that smell made her sick.

Genna put the meat in the refrigerator. With the certain hard core practicality of one who always had to save where she could, she thought that it might be needed for a funeral.

They sat in the living room with the shades drawn against the brightness of the day, and waited. When the telephone finally rang, it was a relief. Genna went to answer it. Ellen heard her say steadily, "Yes," and "All right."

She came back, stood in the doorway, looked at Ellen, and said, as if commenting instead of quoting, "Enoch walked with God: and he was not; for God took him."

After Genna took Ellen away, the others began to file out too, saying little. But Leona Bentley sank back down in her seat, ignoring her husband's urging. She was staring up towards the altar. "The cup is gone," she said.

"You've had a shock," her husband soothed. "You'd better go home and lie down."

"The cup is gone," she repeated, grabbing at her daughter's arm. "The one he drank out of."

Tanya paid no attention. But Max Rourke had heard, and, with a lifting of the eyebrows, moved forward to look. Others followed, stopping at the front seat to watch. He crouched down and, hands on thighs, searched the stretch of carpet running from the altar back under the first pews. "She's right; it is gone," he said, looking up at them, face pale but mocking. "'Fess up, somebody. Now is not the time for petty pilfering." When no one moved or spoke, his brows climbed higher.

He was interrupted by an importantly bustling little man who came up the aisle exclaiming, "What's this I hear about the reverend?"

"Looked like a heart attack, Doctor," Adam Cullen said.

"Nonsense!" the medic snapped, dropping into a pew and fanning himself with a program. "The man was in better health than I am." When they all stared at him, he repeated in an exaggeratedly slow and emphasized tone, *"There was nothing wrong with Enoch Foster's heart."*

A new interest seemed to revive and color Max Rourke's sallow features. "Well, well," he murmured, rising slowly, gaze fluttering hungrily, as Lawson's had done, from one face to another. His arm brushed the bouquets, and the petals of a maroon tulip showered down onto the carpet like spatters of blood.

CHAPTER 2

Behold, I send unto you proph-
ets, and wise men, and
scribes: and some of them ye
shall kill.
Matthew 23:34

State police lieutenant Bill Lansky was in a foul mood that did not accord with the peaceful turquoise of the Easter sky. His wife had pressed him into making an unhabitual appearance in church that morning in a suit that was getting annually smaller. And now, when he should be home, lying in a hammock, enjoying the spring weather, and watching his children hunt colored eggs in the grass, he was on his way to another church to investigate a "suspicious occurrence."

An elderly pastor had keeled over in front of his

congregation after drinking the sacramental wine. Elderly men keeled over every day, and some elderly women for that matter. But in this instance, the cup he drank from seemed to have disappeared.

There would be some simple explanation, but, just in case there wasn't, a ranking officer had better be there. Murder by chalice would cause a journalistic sensation.

Lansky abhorred sensations. His opinion was that religious people caused enough trouble by their stubborn blockading of abortion clinics.

Sergeant Gary Rhys, who accompanied him, seemed unnaturally cheerful. "It's something different," he explained almost eagerly, "than your standard marital disagreement stabbing."

A couple of ushers waited for them in the church, sitting across the aisle from each other in the back seats, as if to distance themselves as much as possible from where *it* had happened. One had a frightened-looking wife with him.

The sanctuary smelled clean: of varnish and wax and oil soap. Their footsteps were muffled by carpet. In the front, the flowers still leaned indifferently over an empty stretch of carpet.

There was always a kind of hush to these places, especially when they were almost empty. Lansky shifted uneasily, looked up at a stained-glass window over the altar. Carrying a lamb over one arm, Christ looked down on them, sad-faced.

The pastor's Bible still lay open on the pulpit, the place marked by a torn piece of paper reading, "Trustees' meeting, 2:00." The book was well worn with many scribbled comments in the margins. No clues there, or, at least, not the kind the lieutenant was looking for.

The ushers were country men with squinty eyes and big calloused hands. Men who came right to the point. "The things were back there," one of them said and pointed to a table in the rear left-hand corner. They all walked back past empty seats. A lot of things had been forgotten by parishioners in the morning's excitement: a leather-covered Bible, a lace purse, a child's construction paper basket with a few smudgy chocolates, and a paper chain of angels. Would Easter be forever tainted for some little one by what had happened here?

The communion things had been returned to the table: little silver cups with sticky traces of juice in their depths, a silver tray with a dusting of crumbs and a few leftover wafers. "My wife and I prepared them," the spokesman continued. He put a reassuring hand on the woman's arm.

They kept the communion set at their home. It was antique, and therefore not to be left in a building whose side doors were usually unlocked. They brought the grape juice with them in a still-sealed bottle, poured it out after they reached the church, put lids over both trays and linen cloths over all. The other usher could vouch for all of this. He and his family arrived at the same time.

21

He had other things to do—posting song numbers, opening the big Bible on its podium to the morning's reading, washing out and filling the pastor's water jug and glass in the kitchen. But his wife stayed and chatted with the other women. She could vouch for what they had—or hadn't—done. She'd taken the children home, but if they wanted to talk to her—

"It can wait," Lansky said—wait to see if an autopsy showed just another heart failure. "And these things were left here right up to the end of the service?"

That was the custom. Both ushers had gone together to get the silver trays. There was no way that one could have inserted anything without the other seeing. There also seemed no way that most of the parishioners could have done it. There were three sections of pews in the church. The main aisle ran straight from the door to the altar between the right and middle sections. Most people went up that way to take their seats. Only those making for the left section would cross by the communion table. And those, it seemed, were few enough.

There were no reserved seats in the church, but people tended to sit in the same places each Sunday anyway. And most of those on the left were "newcomers," those who had come to this village within the last ten years: the Bentleys, Genna Leon, the DeWitts, Adam Cullen, Max Rourke, and Ellen Foster.

Standing by the table, Lansky looked up towards where most of the congregation would have sat. It was possible, just barely possible. The ushers would have been busy greeting people at the door; the nearest would have had his back turned. There was a pillar that blocked off the view of most of those in the main part of the sanctuary. But still it would have involved lifting off a linen cloth and a lid, and that could have been easily observed by anyone in the left section turning their head. And people did turn their heads, look to see who was coming in, extend greetings. Not strictly impossible, but certainly taking a colossal risk.

Someone had picked up the cup in all the excitement, and then forgotten about it, or was afraid now to mention it after such a fuss had been made. Just in case, he took down the names of the newcomers, asked about their relations with their pastor.

Ellen Foster stood just inside the door of her bedroom and viewed her own tightly made bed with dull incomprehension. After a moment or two, she walked across and sat down on the edge of it, and it creaked slightly as it always did. She sat with her hands folded in her lap and her feet neatly together. Enoch was dead, poisoned, and they thought she'd done it.

People had come to offer consolation; their eyes had been evasive, almost guilty, there'd been muttering in corners. It had almost been wrenched into the open when Max Rourke had come to sit beside her and she knew that she had no hope of holding up under his cleverness. "So," he'd said. "What do you think happened to the chalice? Did—"

Genna had stalked across the room, picked up a cup of cold coffee that somebody'd left sitting on a stand, splashed its contents deliberately into Rourke's lap. "Clumsy of me," she'd said. "You'll want to go home and wash that out before it sets up. It was nice of you to come." Genna had her own brand of ruthlessness.

The last six months had been too good to last. *Perhaps,* Ellen thought, *I've known that all along. Perhaps I caused my own end to it.*

There'd been times as a child that she'd been sure of her own innocence, but her aunt had always been so positive of the opposite, that the child would begin to doubt. Would imagine the crime over and over in her head until she was sure it must be memory, not imagination. Until she no longer trusted her own mind which could deceive her so easily.

But on this one, she could not even imagine where she might have gotten the poison, and that confused her. They were all so sure; they must be right. Who else would have any reason for poisoning Enoch? He had lived here peacefully with them for years until her advent.

She sat rigidly upright with light beating down—it seemed heavy on her eyelids—and could not even pray. "Be honest with God," Enoch had said once. "He can tell the difference, you know. Although," he added drily, "some people don't seem to realize that."

But how could she be honest when she no longer knew what the truth was?

She forced herself to go through the mechanical motions of preparing for bed. Genna was staying the night in the guest room across the hall. But the house seemed incredibly still—empty—with only the light and silence beating back the dark from the windows.

She turned on the bedside lamp, turned off the other, sat on the edge of the bed again. Something told her that she should be angry, but all anger had been leached out of her years ago, leaving only fear—fear of being noticed. To blend in, go unremarked, that was safety. And now that was denied her. She was pinned, paralyzed, like a wild animal under headlights. The thought made the light suddenly repugnant, and she switched it off quickly, scurried under a blanket.

But she wouldn't be left any cover for long. What would they do to her if she was the one?

A thud, a movement from the direction of her open window. She jerked up, smashing her head against the headboard. Through a sickening, reeling pain, she groped for the lamp, clutching at empty space, sucking in air in great, painful gulps, the blanket tangling, binding her legs, a new fear drumming like the pain inside her skull; what if she *wasn't* the one?

She finally found the switch, and the lamp tipped

toward her, light exploding in her face, blinding dilated pupils.

A cat. It was Genna's cat. Genna had put it out, but it must have come back up the tree by the window. Now it sat on the sill and regarded Ellen with disfavor. Then it dropped into the room, padded across to the door.

She set the lamp upright, collapsed back against the pillows, shaking. She had been so sure that it was the murderer. Didn't that prove that she couldn't have— She turned her head stiffly from side to side like a blind person, seeking some clue, some sound to provide orientation. Or did it only prove that her mind was even more treacherous than she'd believed?

The cat was watching her expectantly. It wanted Genna probably. She should get up, let it out. But she was still shaking too hard to walk. She shook her head helplessly at it.

It turned suddenly, made a flying leap at the bed. She shrank back, appalled. Did that mean that it was angry? It marched regally over her legs and stomach, stood on her chest, and peered at her face. She didn't dare move, averted her gaze, so as not to antagonize it. It turned around two or three times, pawing at the blanket in an aimless sort of way, then plunked down heavily over her breastbone, so close that its fur almost brushed her cheek. Then it closed its eyes and rumbled. She moved a tentative finger and touched its head. It rumbled harder.

Careful not to disturb it, she stretched out her arm to turn off the lamp again. The animal's warmth and the light vibration of its purr were soothing. Rather like a live heating pad. She closed her eyes and felt a little less alone.

The coroner was very cautious when Lansky called him the next morning. He had decided on ingestion of an alien substance. Just what that alien substance was, he wasn't prepared to say. If he had to guess, probably some type of plant poison. They didn't generally work so quickly, but Foster had been a small man, and plant poisons were notoriously unpredictable. Some of them also left very little trace in the victim's body.

"That," Lansky snarled to Rhys, "is just dandy! A whole lot of help, that is!"

It was also why, on a Monday morning, the two police officers were heading for a village that had always been "well behaved" in the past. It was when the well-behaved ones slipped their leash, Lansky thought, that things got strange.

The day was cold and very wet. Huddled in a protective arc of hills under a glowering sky, the town did not seem to welcome their intrusion.

The wipers strove ineffectually with the water pouring down the windshield as the unmarked police car swung into a driveway beyond a bleary line of yews that

separated the church from the parsonage. An Audi, motor
running, stood in the drive, and Lansky parked beside it.
As he and Sergeant Rhys sprinted toward the door of the
old house, a well-dressed woman emerged, popping open
an umbrella and said, "They're in the kitchen," and plunged
through the downpour towards her car.

She had left the door ajar for them, and they went
on into the hallway. It was dim with warped boards that
gave slightly underfoot and a far-off drumming of rain
on the roof.

Lansky cleared his throat, called self-consciously,
"Anybody home?"

"In here," a female voice said from the left. In there,
two women were sitting at a table, picking at ham and
scrambled eggs. They didn't have any lights on, and the
room had a somber overcast of gray and the smell of
damp wood.

"Good morning," Lansky said. "I'm Lieutenant Bill
Lansky and this is Sergeant Rhys. We're looking for an
Ellen Foster?"

He was staring, mesmerized, at the younger woman,
who seemed to have eyes growing out of her neck. Her
unkempt hair swathed her shoulders like an old-style
furry stole, a fur apparently with the head still attached.
He blinked, and saw that the eyes were those of a dark
cat, the same shade as the hair, perched precariously on
the top of the woman's high-backed chair with its front
paws draped over her shoulder.

She looked up only briefly from her morose stirring of the liquid in her cup. "*Gendarme,*" she said, and went back to watching the ripples as if reading them.

Those ushers had mentioned rumors of the pastor's cousin being "mental," and this seemed conclusive. Then, "Hello, I'm Ellen," the other woman said. She was quite plain and ordinary looking but with something distant about the eyes. "Won't you sit down? This is Genna Leon."

Lansky sat, cautiously. Rhys stood behind him. "Who's John Darm?" the lieutenant asked.

"Men at arms," Ellen said. "French for police, I think."

"Oh, are you French?" Lansky asked Genna, who shook her head without looking up.

"No, I was just showing off," she said. "Did you want anything in particular?"

Determinedly ignoring her, Bill addressed himself to Ellen Foster. "I suppose you've heard that there is some question as to how your cousin died?"

"Yes."

"And what do you think?"

Genna had abandoned the cup and was playing with the sugar, piling up spoonfuls at one end of the bowl just to have it slide down and coalesce with the rest again. Ellen watched the other woman's hands as she said, "My cousin was a good man; I don't think anyone would have wanted to harm him."

"They killed Christ, didn't they?" Genna said.

The simple statement was harsh, shocking in the kitchen of an old house on a rainy Monday morning.

It embarrassed the men. Ellen, however, seemed to consider it matter-of-factly. "Yes," she said finally, "and Stephen, and Paul—"

"And thousands of other saints since," Genna said. "How did he die?"

For a befuddled instant, Lansky wasn't sure who she was talking about. Then, "Alien substance," he muttered.

Ellen looked puzzled.

Genna balanced a knife across the handle of the milk pitcher, picked up a pair of plastic salt and pepper shakers, delicately set one on the haft and one on the blade. The cat's yellow eyes followed her movements. The knife teetered a moment. "He means poison," she said. The haft whacked down, skipping the pepper shaker off onto its side and sending the salt skidding down the table, dropping crystals on its way. Rhys jumped. The cat dug in its claws.

"*Ouch,*" Genna said, and slapped at its paw. "Why so jumpy over a little spilled salt, Sergeant?" she asked. "You aren't superstitious, are you?"

Lansky turned irritably on her. "Since you insist on these interruptions, Miss Leon, what do *you* know about poison?"

She smiled. "Quite a bit actually."

30

Looking worried, Ellen interrupted. "Genna," she explained, "gave a little talk on poisonous plants at one of our recent garden club meetings."

"She did, did she?" Lansky said. "And how many people heard this little talk?"

"Twenty or thirty maybe?" Ellen guessed tentatively.

"And how many more heard of it?" he asked. It was a rhetorical question, since he quickly added another, "And how many had access to any of these plants?"

"I have aconite in my garden," Genna volunteered, swabbing up salt with a damp fingertip. "And foxglove."

"You *grow* poisonous plants?"

"If I left flowers out just because they were toxic," the artist said mildly, "I would have to eliminate delphiniums, larkspur, daffodils, lily of the valley—" She licked her finger like a child, and the cat stared from her shoulder. "Bleeding heart, rhododendron, just to name a few. But, as I also pointed out in my talk, all this murder mystery stuff about using plants to kill people is mostly a lot of hooey. It's impossible to predict exactly how much of any one plant will kill any one person. And to get the poison in any sort of concentrated form, you would need to have a still and know how to use it. So, if we're talking about a plant alkaloid here, I'd recommend you look at medicines that already contain the stuff. In small amounts, these plants can cure as well as they kill, you know. Though I don't think they use aconite any-more; it was just too nasty."

She smiled sweetly at the policemen. "I'd think digitalis would have been a much safer bet myself. Made from foxglove. Easier to get hold of, and it would have looked much more like a heart attack."

"Did *you* know the Reverend Foster very well, Miss Leon?" Lansky asked.

She raised her eyebrows. "He was my minister."

"Nothing else?"

"We were good friends, I think you could say."

"And just how friendly were you?"

Her ever-restless fingers had been playing with the cross around her neck. They stilled momentarily as the obvious implications of that sunk in. Ellen made a feeble movement of protest. Genna's lips quirked. "Never mind, Ellen. The police are paid to have filthy minds. Our relationship was strictly platonic, Lieutenant. Being interpreted—spiritual. Nothing more."

"Even so," Lansky continued doggedly, "you might have resented the entrance of another woman onto the scene. There might have been some . . . rivalry for the pastor's attention?"

The two women stared at him and at each other, dumbfounded. Then Genna began to laugh. Ellen joined in, with more than a hint of hysteria.

"Because we're repressed old spinsters, I suppose," Genna choked. "With nothing better to do than run after a man twice our age. You amaze me, Mr. Lansky. I thought your kind of chauvinism went out with the horse and buggy."

Ellen had gone from hysteria to red-faced anger. "I can't believe," she said in a stilted, quivery tone, "that you could so denigrate the memory of a man like my cousin by even implying—" Here, her voice failed. The sergeant shifted uncomfortably.

"I'm sure Lieutenant Lansky didn't mean to imply anything," he said. "I mean, we just have to ask certain things—"

"We don't apologize for doing our job," Bill cut in, furious. "A man has been murdered here, and if you consider your comfort more important than finding out who did it—"

"We never consider our comfort more important than the loss of human life," Genna said. She leaned back against her furry headrest, and it purred with incongruous contentment. "Which is why we march, and chain ourselves to lightposts in front of clinics. I thought I'd seen you somewhere before, Lieutenant. But never mind." With deceptive softness, *"We know that you were just doing your job."*

Lansky got up from his chair and left the room without another word. Making a bemused kind of gesture with shrugged shoulders and palms up, Rhys muttered, "I'm sorry about your cousin, Miss Foster. Bill usually isn't this touchy. I don't know why— Well, sorry." He followed his superior out.

Genna went down the hall after them, and stood in the open doorway to watch them leave. The rain was still coming down with a steady monotony, and the car lurched backward through puddles, spattering itself with mud. Crossing her arms against the dank chill, she considered that she'd brought that off pretty well. The police had been bound to suspect Ellen, the person closest to the victim—and not just the police. She'd seen those meaningful glances the night before too. If it had to be murder, if it had to be one of them, they preferred that it be Ellen—the unknown, the "mental" one, in whom it might be excused.

"If anything ever happens to me," Enoch had said to Genna once, "look after Ellen, will you?"

She had warned him then that it was like setting the blind to lead the blind.

But she was doing her best, in her own convoluted way, having succeeded in shifting official attention from the other to herself, in making Ellen look like the calmer, more ordinary one. *Lansky will implicate me now, if he can. Let him try. I, at least, have a family to back me up.* She imagined a confrontation between her mother and the lieutenant, and smiled. *Ellen doesn't have anybody. Except an uncle caught up in the middle of an African revolution.* He probably wouldn't even get the telegram they'd sent till after the funeral.

Why did you have to go getting yourself murdered anyway, Enoch? We need you. Okay, God, I guess it's just You and us now. Maybe we did overly rely on the reverend, but he knew You so much better. I guess that's going to have to change, huh?

She closed the door and went back inside, almost tripping over the cat who'd followed her down the passageway. "And you, Grimm," she whispered. "You lent a nicely Gothic air to the proceedings, didn't you?"

Ellen had sat through most of the interview with her hands out of sight in her lap. When Genna came back into the kitchen, the other woman was attempting to gather up the dirty breakfast dishes. Those hands were shaking so hard that the china clattered.

"Here, let me do that," Genna ordered, and Ellen subsided back into her seat.

"You're much too obedient, you know that?" the artist asked as she dumped the dishes into the sink. "I'll make us some chamomile tea; I think we both need it after our grilling."

She put the kettle on, turned, leaning against the stovefront. "We really should cry. We'd feel better."

"I know. I can't."

"Me neither." Genna sat down, pulled a comb from one capacious pocket, and set to work on her hair. "But I suppose that worrying about not crying is worse for us than not crying."

"I just remembered," Ellen said suddenly. "You couldn't have put poison in the cup. You brought that bouquet of daffodils, and you took them straight down the main aisle to the altar. Then you went across the

front to get to your seat. I'd better call and tell them."
She started up again.

"Sit!" Genna said sternly. "I've always wanted to be
a mystery woman and you're ruining my big chance.
Besides, somebody else will be sure to mention it."

Ellen sat. "If you're sure. I can't believe the things
that man said—"

"He would have said more," Genna said, "if he'd
known about the money Enoch gave me once." Screw-
ing up her face in concentration, she started a braid at
the back of her head. "It was about a year after I got
here. I gave up a good job in town for this, you know.
My family disapproved. But I didn't think I should
spend the only life I have doing something I hated. So
when Uncle Leon left me his farm and a little bit of
money, I took it as some kind of sign, and moved on
out here."

She finished the braid, jammed it into a ruthless knot
at the back of her head, crisscrossing it with hairpins, and
got up to retrieve the squealing kettle. "A year later, I was
completely broke. I've never been good with money,
and I'm afraid I got carried away—on the garden in
particular. Anyway, I knew I was going to have to give it
all up, and I was a bit low, as you can imagine. All the
bills were due, and there was nothing to pay them with.
Frankly, it was the worst time of my life. I didn't even
think I was getting through to God." Grimm had returned to the back of her chair. A strand of hair had

already worked itself loose from her bun, and every time she moved her head, he swatted at it.

She poured hot water, and the sweet, soothing smell of chamomile rose with the steam. "Then Enoch came stomping along like the angel Gabriel, read me a lecture on the arrogance of a pride that refuses to ask for help, and dumped an envelope full of cash in my lap. I still don't know how he knew; I suppose God told him." On one of his passes, Grimm got his claws caught in her hair. As she turned her head to look at him, he was almost dragged off his precarious balance, jerking frantically to get his other paw back. He succeeded barely, and, looking complacent, began to lick the sullied paw. The mangled bun let go in a shower of pins. She reached back over her shoulder and gave the cat a shove. He landed on the floor hissing outrage and glared malevolently up at her.

Cradling the teacup between her palms, she smiled at a memory. "He always paid attention, you know. To other people as well as to God. Maybe that's why God always found it so easy to get through to him. Most of us just don't pay attention."

The two police officers rode in silence down a well-graveled lane that had branched off the road almost opposite the church drive. They were headed for Adam Cullen's farm. The homes of the suspects were located in a loose circle around the church.

Cullen's farm was to the north of the main road. The church was set on a corner between the blacktop and a dirt road that ran to the south, passing the DeWitt's place. Max Rourke's home was west of the village on the main road, and the Bentley's big house stood high on a hill to the east.

Where the lane forked, the police car veered left, still on the gravel, into a neat farmyard and, pulled up in front of a small house trailer whose lighted windows glowed a watery yellow through the streaming rain. At the end of the right fork, they'd been told, was Genna Leon's place. Lansky didn't move, waiting for the deluge to subside, and Rhys said, "You blew it, Bill."

The lieutenant glowered at the windshield and didn't reply.

"You better watch that temper. What's the matter with you anyway? This guy wasn't one of those TV evangelists who make a six-figure salary and do a bit of extorting and fornicating on the side. He was over seventy years old, for goodness' sake! And he spent most of those years at the same little church.

"We went there to question his cousin, and what happens? You end up spouting off at somebody entirely different just because she was on good terms with her pastor and has a certain plant in her garden? You have a fight with your wife or something?"

"Yes," his superior said unexpectedly. "Nance has got herself involved with a bunch of radicals like those two. You wouldn't like it if your wife was in love with religion either!" Lansky climbed out of the car to plod through an unremitting downpour to the trailer. Raising his eyebrows and forming a silent whistle, Rhys followed.

Adam Cullen was working on production records on his computer. He was a big man who seemed almost to fill his little home. Any space left over was taken up by the black and white collie that lay on the floor. The young farmer's organizational talents apparently did not extend to housekeeping. Dirty dishes filled the sink, and farm magazines were scattered over a sagging sofa and scuffed coffee table. The two policemen sat gingerly on the sofa, having to lean forward to counteract its downward pull. Cullen straddled the chair in front of the computer, crossing his brawny arms over its back and resting his chin on one big fist.

Yes, he was one of those who'd tried to revive Reverend Foster. No, poison had never occurred to him at the time. No, there had been no obvious smell that he could recall, but they should really ask the one who'd done the mouth-to-mouth, who would have been more likely to notice.

He supposed that Ellen Foster would inherit whatever the pastor had left, which would probably be precious little. Enoch had been—a dry hint of disapproval?—a very generous man. There was a small life insurance policy, he thought, probably not much more than enough to bury him. They should ask Garth DeWitt who did the church's books and had also helped the pastor fill out his income tax forms. Garth would be more likely to know Foster's financial condition.

Yes, Adam had heard the rumors that Ellen Foster was "mental," but had never seen any signs of it himself. "I mind my own business, Lieutenant," he said, "and hope others will do the same."

"You don't picket abortion clinics then?"

"No. I've never seen that it does much good."

"You know Genna Leon?"

A hint of a rueful grin. "My neighbor." The farmer made a gesture with his thumb. "Down the right fork there."

"You know that she has some poisonous plants in her garden?"

"She has lots of plants." Caution.

"Are you an educated man, Mr. Cullen?"

"I have an agricultural degree."

"Take any chemistry?"

"Some."

"How about botany? Could you identify poisonous plants on sight?"

Cullen rubbed his chin restively. "I run my cows on pasture during the summer, Lieutenant. I've made it a point to be able to identify the nastier weeds. I wouldn't be as familiar with garden plants."

"You wouldn't be able to pick out something like, say, aconite or digitalis?"

A pause. "Monkshood and foxglove, right?"

"So you do know them?"

"People are gardening-mad around here; you tend to pick up things. I probably couldn't tell unless they were blooming. It's a little early for that yet."

"What about Miss Leon? Was she friendly with the pastor?"

"Yes. They got along well. They read a lot of the same books. Stuff like that."

"Was that all there was to the relationship?" Lansky asked, ignoring Rhys' patent disapproval. "Just friends?"

"What else would there be?"

"What's your relationship with Miss Leon?" Lansky parried. "You're both single and near the same age. Are you just friends too?"

"I think anyone could tell you," Cullen came back, "that my relations with my neighbor tend to be a bit on the cool side. Though what relevance that has to your investigation, I fail to see."

"Perhaps you thought Miss Leon was a bit too friendly with Foster; perhaps you were jealous."

Giving a short, scornful laugh, the farmer said, "So I stole a bit of aconite from her garden and magically transformed it—with my sinister knowledge of chemistry—into a deadly potion for my elderly rival? I never knew cops had such good imaginations." He half-rose. "If that's all—"

Rhys broke in apologetically. "If you don't mind a

couple more minutes, Mr. Cullen. Could you give me your opinion of the following people and which might have had some kind of grudge against your pastor?" He read, "Garth DeWitt, Meredith DeWitt, Elliot Bentley, Leona Bentley, Tanya Bentley, Max Rourke, Ellen Foster, Genna Leon."

"I don't know that any of them had any grudge against Foster," Adam said, "except Max Rourke. He hated him."

Rhys perked to avid attention. "And just why was that?"

"Who knows? You talk about Ellen Foster being 'mental.' Max Rourke is a lot further around the bend than she is.

"The others are just your typical decent ordinary sort. Except Genna, whom I wouldn't call precisely ordinary."

Sergeant Rhys got the picture. This was the minding his own business Cullen had been talking about earlier. Anything else he knew to the detriment of his fellow parishioners, he would keep to himself.

"And will Foster's death make any difference to you?" the sergeant concluded.

Cullen seemed more hesitant over this question than he had over any of the others. He turned his head to look at one of the windows. "I wouldn't have thought so, but—"

Rhys waited patiently. Cullen's fingers twitched.

"Nothing tangible. It's just—he used to pray for us, you know. For all of us."

He gave a short, embarrassed laugh. "I know this isn't the kind of thing you mean." He rose, and they got up too. The computer screen glowed and hummed prosaically behind him. "But he kind of kept us balanced, and things seem to have been thrown off somehow. There's a suspicion—an ugliness. Like maybe we don't know each other as well as we thought we did." He looked at them with something close to dislike. "We were pretty peaceful here. But now you guys are going to be poking and prodding around—stirring up whatever mud you can find. And Enoch's gone. It's kind of like being left . . . unprotected."

And there come in those that
are unlearned, or unbelievers,
will they not say that ye are
mad?
I Corinthians 14:23

Max Rourke had apparently been hunched over a computer as well. He let the two police officers in, waved vaguely at seats. Then he stalked back over to the console, stood glaring at the screen a moment, swore, and stabbed at a button. With a chittering sound, the screen went blank.

His home was almost as sparsely furnished as Cullen's, but here it seemed to be for deliberate effect. The furniture was stark, modern, and, Lanksy discovered, quite as uncomfortable as it looked. The color scheme was gray and white.

Rourke plunked down on a high stool. "Well, gentlemen," he drawled. "I suppose it's about the late Reverend Foster. I do feel some sympathy—for his murderer."

When that elicited no noticeable change in their demeanors, he looked almost sulky, like an adolescent, Lansky thought, whose attempts to shock are met with adult indifference. The lieutenant had never read any of Rourke's novels. His wife had tried one once. From what she had said about it, he wouldn't have expected the author to be the church-going type.

"I suppose you wonder what I was doing there," Rourke persevered. "I mean, it isn't my usual . . . sphere, you know."

Rhys, who had taken a dislike to the other man on sight, looked surprised because he knew it would annoy. "Really?" he said.

Rourke's hands clenched on his knees. "I just find it entertaining," he said—not sounding entertained— "what people will do—will put up with—for the sake of an outmoded superstition." His voice had been growing thinner and tenser. Now he seemed to iron it out with an effort. "Down-to-earth people should know better."

One of those intellectuals, Rhys thought, *who condescend to identify themselves with the common man, and are surprised when the common man isn't grateful.* Since Lansky was

46

silent, the sergeant began. "You had a personal dislike for the minister?" he asked.

"That's right."

"And was this feeling mutual?"

Rourke's jaw clenched. "No," he said finally. "They're not allowed to hate people."

"Well, just what *was* his attitude towards you then?"

The phone rang. Rourke reached a long arm to pluck up the receiver. "I told you I was working on it," he said. Then, voice rising, "No, I haven't started on a new one. You're going to take this one or you're through! Get me?" He slammed the receiver down, managed a smile. "My agent. Thinks he's a critic. Where were we?"

His voice was drawn too tight again for the casual air he was trying to pull off.

"You've finished another book then, Mr. Rourke," Lansky intervened abruptly. "I hear you get your inspiration from acquaintances."

"Yeah." Rourke managed a taut smile. "This one was about Foster, though I'm not allowed to say that. Lawsuits, you know."

"You think he would have sued."

The writer went strangely still. "No. He wouldn't."

Lansky persevered. "He would have been upset then?"

"No."

Rhys glanced curiously at his superior. What was he getting at?

"How *would* he have reacted, Mr. Rourke?" Lansky seemed obsessed with the question.

Staring into space, Rourke said, "He would have been sorry for me."

"Sorry for you?"

"He said—" The outrage spilled into Rourke's voice, causing him to start and stammer in his haste, "he said th-that I was too much of an idealist. An idealist!" The horror in the writer's voice would have been almost funny, if it weren't so compelling. Rourke shook his head bewilderedly. "You just couldn't get at him. Do you know how hard it is to insult someone who hasn't got any sense of dignity at all?"

"You understand, Mr. Rourke," Lansky said. "We're trying to get some objective picture of the man. All the people we've spoken to so far seemed fond of him, and we need to see the other side. Now what is it you're trying to say? In simple terms, please. That he was naive?"

"Oh, no, *no!*" The other shook his head vehemently. "It was impossible to shock him. He'd say that, even if he hadn't heard it all, God had. And that sin tended to be kind of banal anyway. He always talked about God like that. In a matter-of-fact way like there was no question—" Rourke choked, shook his head, lunged up, and began to pace.

"Then I don't understand," Lansky said, "just what it was that you disliked about the man. Unless—" as if suddenly struck by inspiration "it was that you couldn't get at him, that he wouldn't react. Maybe because your public is beginning to fail to react too, *aren't they, Mr. Rourke?*"

The writer stopped and stood still. Then he turned. Sweat was standing out on his forehead, and his hands were shaking.

Rhys tensed. His lieutenant had been deliberately prodding the man, he knew, shoving at a balance as precarious as Genna Leon's cat on the back of a chair. Only the cat could land on its feet.

Rourke controlled himself this time. "Psychology, Lieutenant?" he sneered. "That maybe I killed the man as a sort of scapegoat. And just who was it that I was trying to get at by it? My public? My parents maybe. That's always a favorite."

"Or God," Rhys suggested.

Both of the other men stared at him. "God, Sergeant?" Rourke laughed. "And why would I need to get at someone who doesn't exist?"

"That's a good question," Rhys came back. "Why *would* you? You know your Shakespeare, I presume." Feeling a little smug, the sergeant continued, "Methinks you doth protest too much. Perhaps you found the Reverend Foster just too convincing."

The wind rose; the house shuddered. Somewhere a door banged. Rourke started at the sound. "And for that I killed him?"

"They killed Christ, didn't they?" the sergeant said.

It was definitely not a routine interrogation. Something was putting the two cops almost as much on edge as their suspect: perhaps the thick oppressive dampness, the restless murmurings of wind and rain at the windows, or just the stubborn refusal of the case to assume even the vaguest of shapes.

Unlike Cullen, Max Rourke did not hesitate to disparage his neighbors. He sneered at Adam as the "new breed of yuppie farmer," pasted the same "materialistic" label on the DeWitts. Meredith "never had an original thought in her life," and made a cult of "keeping up with the Joneses"—in this case the Bentleys. He'd made her the central butt of one of his books, and she'd never even realized it. She wouldn't have hesitated to help ease Foster out if she'd been dissatisfied with him, but he rather thought she would find murder to be "in poor taste, definitely lower class." Garth was "her android— no separate life there at all."

The Bentleys were "nauseatingly soap opera." The wealthy business man putting up with an alcoholic wife and rebellious daughter. "It's been way overdone."

He doubted that Ellen Foster had the "substantiality" for homicide. "The typical parasite. If it kills the 'host plant,' it kills itself."

One would have expected him to look more favorably on Genna Leon, who could certainly be categorized as neither materialist nor conformist, but he saved his most scathing commentary for her. She had a little raw talent, he had to admit, but she had "sold out." Her work was derivative, her manner childishly self-indulgent and hopelessly regressive. One of those who didn't have the strength to face the godless future, so weltered romantically in the religion-opiated past. Probably too sentimental for murder—certainly too scatter-brained.

Sergeant Rhys could understand why Rourke's public was tiring of him. He left his listeners drained, depressed. Yet his characterizations didn't make the people he described as banal as he seemed to find them. Rather, they brought them to disturbing life—almost too much so—as people one wouldn't mind watching on TV, but would find tiring in reality.

Already, the two police officers were finding them exhausting. Neither of the DeWitts were at home. It was around noon when Lansky decided abruptly to return and interview Ellen Foster again—separately this time. *He still has hopes of this being a simple one,* Rhys thought.

They found her in the kitchen again, eating lunch. Another woman was with her: a chunky type with an abrupt manner whom Lansky classified immediately as a retired schoolteacher. When he asked if she would mind leaving the room while they talked to Ellen, her answer was "Yes, I do mind. Ellen isn't used to this kind of thing—" as if she herself endured murder investigations every day—"and I think somebody should be with

51

her. To remind her that she doesn't have to answer anything she doesn't want to." And, with a challenging glare and flounce, the "warder" took up position behind Ellen's chair.

"I'm glad you came back," Ellen started off at once when they'd barely sat down. "I wanted to tell you that Genna couldn't have done it."

It was not, for Lansky, a good beginning. Having the chief suspect defending someone else was oddly deflating. Not to mention the intense, unwavering scrutiny of the "guard," who probably knew the Bill of Rights by heart.

Lansky continued with a dogged series of direct, sometimes impertinent questions, but his heart wasn't in it. Ellen answered everything without complaint, though her voice tended to falter over references to her cousin or to the aunt she had lived with earlier. The picture emerged clearly of a girl dominated and terrorized from her earliest years. Neurotic, she must once have been; she could hardly have helped it. But she seemed well on the road to recovery after only six months with the Reverend Foster. That, Lansky had to admit to Rhys after they left, said a lot for the man.

"And it means," Rhys reminded, "that she'd be the last person in the world to want to kill him."

Lansky was not happy with Genna Leon's alibi, but it had been corroborated by the other woman, and there would be others who would probably remember if asked. They bumped down Genna's section of the lane to view the artist in her home environment. A goat on a much-mended chain and a horse in a muddy corral viewed them with interest. The house was a sagging wooden type, stained a dark gray by the rain.

They found her also eating lunch in a large room where the damp mingled strangely with a strong odor of linseed oil and turpentine and where their heads brushed hanging bunches of musty smelling herbs as they entered. They stopped involuntarily to gape. A potbellied stove in the center of the room emitted a ferocious heat. Dried plants were strung randomly about the room. Flats of live seedlings occupied every available space by the windows. The rest of the room seemed to undulate in gentle waves of chaos. Books and papers were piled randomly on chairs, table, floor, and sofa, some having toppled, some seeming close to it. Genna was perched on a high stool in front of an easel, dried-looking paint tubes scattered round its base. Legs twined casually around those of the stool, she was consuming what looked to be salad from a big bowl in her lap. It was a peculiar mixture of greenery anyhow. "Siddown," she muttered crunchily, gesturing with her fork.

This was easier said than done. Lansky finally plucked the cat off one stack, transferred the stack gingerly to a bare spot on a table, and discovered a chair seat. Rhys wisely chose to stand.

"What *is* that?" he asked.

"Herbs mostly," she said. "'S what I eat when I'm low on groceries."

"Aren't you afraid you might get them mixed up sometime with—"

"Aconite, for instance?" she finished for him. "I don't plant stuff like that with the edibles. Of course, some of them do self-sow." She poked rather dubiously at what remained in the bottom of the bowl. "No, that's caraway—I think."

"Ipecac," she added cheerfully, shoving the bowl onto the edge of a stand containing her palette and pointing to a bottle. "Doctor said I should get it after I absentmindedly swallowed turpentine for tea. Can't use it for turpentine, of course, but he thought I should have it around—for other emergencies." She picked up another dish containing a baked apple, began pouring thick clotted cream over it.

Lansky viewed this with something like horror. "Haven't you ever heard of cholesterol?"

She gave him a mischievous look, muttered, "The modern strengthening of minor morals."

"What?"

"Chesterton. He said the more that people let major morals go, the more they insist on good habits. Like killing unborn children is okay, but eating beef is a cardinal sin."

Lansky chose to ignore that.

"I'm sorry I can't offer you gentlemen lunch," she

continued chattily. "I keep some hens out in the barn, so I have lots of eggs, but we know about eggs, don't we?"

"This isn't a game, Miss Leon," the lieutenant snapped. "A man has been murdered here."

"I know," she said. She moved a little on the stool so they could see the canvas behind her. "It was meant to be a surprise for him."

In the painting, a man looked up from his desk, from the Bible in front of him, a quirky smile on his face, an irrepressible twinkle. An old man, yes, as seen by the light blazing through white hair, but what struck one was youth and buoyancy. Not the lightness of triviality, but of one released from triviality. "It took him seventy-some years to get that way," Genna said softly, "and he was a natural. None of us are likely to get close, but, as he used to say, half the fun's in the trying."

Lansky brought them sternly back to earth. "He seems to have been a better sort than most, granted, Miss Leon, but somebody had reason to kill him. Read her the list, Sergeant."

Genna wiped a smear of cream from her upper lip. "Not Ellen certainly," she said, when Rhys had finished. "If you'd seen her face— And not Adam; he did his level best to save him. I think he was as fond of Enoch as he is of anybody. And Adam just isn't"—she fumbled with her spoon searching for the right word—"extreme enough for murder. He can't even bring himself to be openly rude until he loses his temper. This cream, for instance, is his. He told me, when I first moved here,"—her brows arched ruefully—"when he didn't know me very well, that I could take any milk I needed from his tank. He's never withdrawn the offer, because it would be impolite to do so; fortunately it's never occurred to him when he was in a real rip-roaring rage. He might, perhaps, hit somebody a little too hard in one of those spells, but poison—no. That would be a little too stagy for his tastes."

The cat had not appreciated being removed from its perch. It sat on the floor, eyes slitted, tail twitching, laying, Rhys thought, a heavy hex on the lieutenant. Then it deliberately turned its back on the newcomers, stalked with offended dignity across to Genna's stool, gave a single imperious mer-aww. She reached down for it without shifting her gaze.

"Meredith is okay after you get used to her. She puts a little too much emphasis on the looks of things. She can be critical, but she isn't cruel. I mean she really does it for the other person's good. She isn't like people who just say that that's the reason. Perhaps we get along because we have entirely different goals, so we're not competing in any sense. I can't see her killing anyone; after all, what would the neighbors think?" The cat draped itself across her knees with fluid grace, and she rubbed it under the chin.

"Garth is nice, but weak. I doubt he'd kill a mosquito unless told to.

"Elliot Bentley is your average worried businessman. I suppose everybody's been telling you that Leona drinks, but I'm not too sure about that. She's always been fairly lucid when I've seen her, though she does stay in a lot. Very gentle, eager to please. The daughter has hit the rebel years, but she's a sensible child; I think she'll come out of it all right. I can't see any of them doing it." She had absently stopped stroking the cat, and it responded by turning its head and nipping at her finger. Genna smacked it lightly and dumped it off her lap without changing her distantly thoughtful expression.

"Max Rourke is, frankly, a bore. One of these people who adore *art* in capital letters as an end in itself, which is the sheerest nonsense. And it's only art to him if it's ugly and depressing and most people hate it. That allows him to feel a little superior, you see.

"Though Enoch did think that Max was close to some kind of breakthrough or breakdown. He said he wouldn't be surprised if Max converted. I think Enoch was kind of working on it, in fact."

At their incredulous expressions, she laughed. "You think it's so impossible? Look at St. Paul. His favorite hobby at one time was imprisoning Christians and having them put to death.

"But being so obsessed with Christ, even if on the wrong side, was dangerous to him. And God isn't too picky about how He gets you, you know. Unscrupulous, C. S. Lewis called him. Lewis was an atheist to begin with too.

"Anyway, that could have backfired if Max really went off the rails instead. He's an idealist; only an idealist can be that mad at the world when it doesn't live up to his expectations. Yes, I think Max probably is extreme enough for murder." She looked back at the portrait. "I would prefer to think that it was for something like that that Enoch died. He would have considered the possibility worth the risk."

She turned toward them again, whipped up a rock from the stand beside her and hurled it. *At* them, Rhys thought confusedly, but it went well wide, bouncing off a wall behind them. A squeak and a scuttling. Lansky was out of his chair, and both men's hands hovered in the vicinity of their revolvers. "Rats," Genna muttered.

Her attention veered back to their faces. She blinked and laughed. "Sorry, gentlemen. I meant rats literally," she explained. "The place is overrun with them." The cat, looking bored, began to wash a paw. "I've been trying to scare them off, but it isn't working. They're only getting bolder. I guess I'll have to resort to poison."

Lansky was—predictably—boiling after that interview. "She did it all right!" he snarled. "I don't know how, but any woman who keeps an animal like that—" the lieutenant was not fond of even the most well-behaved cats—"and goes around whaling rocks at mice is capable of anything! If she thinks I'm going to be fooled by that wide-eyed act—"

Sergeant Rhys had a pretty good idea of what Genna Leon's game was. But a wise subordinate never pointed out where his superior was being led by the nose.

There was no one home at the Bentley mansion either. Or at least no one answered the door.

The two police officers drove back to town and, after stopping for a little lunch of their own, on to the office where Meredith DeWitt worked. It was the headquarters of a women's magazine catering to the upper middle class. In the thickly carpeted hush of its waiting room, the men leafed through copies of the periodical while the receptionist pushed buttons and spoke in a modulated voice to a speaker on her console. The magazine was like the receptionist and the room: slick, impeccably groomed, with an understated elegance. Meredith DeWitt, who came out to greet them and to lead them back to her office, fit right in. She was the woman they'd seen leaving Ellen Foster's house that morning when they were arriving.

She sat across a desk from them and expressed her dismay over the Reverend Foster's untimely passing in well-rounded syllables. Was she to understand from their presence that there was after all some irregularity— a crease in her normally smooth forehead implied that irregularity was to be avoided at all costs. Rather like the laxative companies, Rhys thought, and, ashamed of this irreverent comparison, he squirmed and looked at his fingernails which suddenly seemed cruddy.

She had been on good terms with the pastor, but hadn't really known him that well. "He was of another generation, and"—a shrug—"our interests tended to differ." She knew nothing about poisons. "It doesn't come up much in my line of work." She did have a garden. From her attitude, it was easy to guess that she wasn't particularly enthusiastic about it, but that gardens were *de rigueur* now. There was a man who came around once a week to take care of it.

She was a little more cautious than others had been in her appraisals of her fellow suspects, as one keeping a weather eye on the possibility of libel suits.

This was especially true in her commentary on Ellen. "One doesn't like to be judgmental, but the woman doesn't really *do* anything." Doing things was apparently important to Meredith. "I mean, it can't be healthy." There was no actual declaring that Ellen was unfit mentally—only a slight raising of the eyebrows.

She found it predictable that Genna should take the other under her wing. "Genna—" a tolerant smile, "is the type that nurses sick animals. Always for the underdog." That attitude, the smile seemed to say, was commendable but not practical. Genna had been better friends with the pastor. "I'm afraid I don't take my religion quite as extremely as she does, Lieutenant." She was amused at the idea that there might have been anything else to the relationship. "Genna is morally rather . . . shall we say, stringent."

Her indulgent shrug implied that she herself was a little more open-minded. *How open-minded does one have to be,* Rhys wondered, *to wink at murder?* It all came down, he supposed, to situational ethics. An eminent German theologian was supposed to have conspired in a plot to assassinate Hitler and had been hanged for it. He entertained himself with speculating what would impel each of the suspects he'd seen so far to murder. Cullen, he thought, would kill for his farm, Rourke for revenge, and Genna for an ideal; she wouldn't have hesitated in dispatching Hitler. Despite her position as chief suspect, he couldn't imagine Ellen Foster raising the initiative for murder. It would take, he thought, a certain brazenness to step outside the social norm that far. Or callousness.

"—a wicked temper though," Meredith DeWitt was saying when he focused on her again. "But usually he keeps it well under control." The warmth in her voice approved of control. "And one can't really blame him. Genna can be irksome, you must admit."

Although he didn't express his vigorous agreement with that, Lansky finally found himself relaxing a little. Here was a sensible witness at last. The first he'd encountered—with the possible exception of Cullen—

who wasn't a bubble or two off plumb. "Quite successful," Meredith summed up Adam.

She was a little evasive about Max Rourke. "A brilliant mind, of course. He and the pastor had their disagreements, but I'm sure it was all just"—her hand flapped—"religion, you know."

Just religion! Rhys thought ironically. Just religion had been and was still responsible for a lot of spilled blood. Of course, maybe you could say a lack of religion was responsible for a lot more— It was warm in the office, rain still whispered at the windows.

Elliot Bentley was "a saint really. The way he puts up with that wife and daughter of his." But she seemed reluctant to enter specific criticisms against the females in question. "Only one would think, with all that money—"

Meredith seemed to believe that, if one was rich, it was the rankest ingratitude not to be content.

Deciding reluctantly that there was little more to be learned from her, Lansky rose, kicked the ankle of his sergeant, who appeared to be dozing. Rhys jerked up and—he had just been dreaming of his army days— stood rigidly to attention

"Oh, Lieutenant," Meredith said when they were almost to the door, "I suppose that someone mentioned about my being late getting into the service that morning"

He stopped and turned "Well, no, actually—"

"Yes, I'd volunteered to help pass out some candy we ladies made for the children. We didn't have our regular Sunday school that morning, so the children had theirs downstairs while the rest of us were having church. My husband and I usually sit in the left block, but that day he took a seat towards the back of the middle section so that I could join him quietly when I was done. Though I suppose it isn't important." Despite the inquiring innocence of that look, Lansky suspected that she knew just how important it really was.

Garth DeWitt was out of his office and his secretary didn't know when he would be back, so the two policemen returned to Deerfield.

At the Bentley place again, they still got no response to their knocking. The house was big and white with pillars, and was set on a hill above the village. Despite its grandeur, it had a shut-up air—as if the curtains were always drawn, as if the terrace was never used.

As they were turning away, a motorcycle roared up the circular drive and pulled up behind their car with a spray of gravel The driver was a shaggy teenage boy The passenger wore a helmet. The latter dismounted, re moved the helmet, shook back her hair, and regarded them sardonically "The cops, I presume?" she said, handing the helmet to the driver without looking at him

Then, almost as an afterthought as she started up the drive, "Thanks, Kev."

Face sulky, Kev, dangling the helmet from the handlebars, revved the cycle into action again, veering around the police car to shoot down the far end of the drive. "Born to be wild," Tanya said in amused commentary, and, to the policemen, "Well, come on in."

"Your mother doesn't seem to be home," Lansky commented as they followed her to the door and she inserted a key.

She flashed him that half-mocking look again over one shoulder. "Oh, she's here; she's always here."

Throwing open the door, the girl raised her voice. "You'll have to come out of hiding, Ma! It's the law!"

It was dim inside. A door closed somewhere on the second floor. Movement in the hallway up there resolved itself into a slender form at the top of the stairs. "Really, Tanya!" the woman said. And, to the two men, in amused exasperation as she descended, "Teenagers!"

She led them into a front room that looked as unused as the rest of the house, gestured them to seats on the sofa, sat down across from them on a straight-backed chair "I suppose it's about Reverend Foster A great tragedy"

Looked at more closely, she seemed too thin, and her casual tone was belied by the fingers she twisted together in her lap

"Yes," he said, "I'm Lieutenant Lansky, and this is "

He paused. She had started convulsively at the name, cast him what could only be termed a wild look. He could feel also a sudden stillness—tension—in the teenager standing behind them. "Is something wrong?"

"Oh, no." Leona's mouth twisted in the travesty of a smile. "Nothing at all." Her nervous glance seemed to beseech her daughter.

"Lansky," Tanya said, moving with a jerk. "That wouldn't be William Lansky, by any chance?"

"Yes, it is." He turned to look at her. "Why?"

Only Rhys saw Leona frantically shaking her head at the girl.

"Would your wife's name be Nancy?"

"That's right." Lansky was puzzled and uneasy. "Why?"

A wry little smile. "Because your wife is my mother's sister. Nice to finally meet you . . . *Uncle* Bill."

Our flesh had no rest, but we were troubled on every side; without were fightings, within were fears.
II Corinthians 7:5

After the two policemen left, Max Rourke could not settle down to work again. Instead he paced up and down his long room, staring out at the rain.

Your public is failing to react. And, according to his agent, they would fail to react to this one too. Why? When he himself reacted more strongly every day. When his passion against what he repudiated literally cost him food and sleep, caused his hands to shake like an alcoholic's. Why couldn't they see the danger of men like Foster? And why couldn't he let this alone?

Perhaps the sergeant had been partly right. It didn't feel anymore like he was exposing a myth, but like he was fighting something much more substantial. He knew enough of psychology to be sure that it was only his mind creating this opposite to give itself an outlet for its rage. But he also knew enough to realize that his obsession was becoming dangerous.

The only way to make it disappear was to let go of all this—go back to the city for a little rest, hook up with some of the old crowd. He'd come to the country for simplicity; he laughed mirthlessly at the thought. And then something unbidden in him screamed at Foster, and at the vague shape behind, *Why can't you stay dead?*

Ellen wandered into the living room. She had drifted from room to room all morning. The windows always drew her, and she went, almost compulsively, to look out at the relentless rain. If only she could go outside; things would seem so much better if only she could get out.

She turned wearily away, gaze sweeping the room for something with which to occupy a few minutes. Her purse was sitting on the floor beside the sofa. She would tidy that up.

She gathered it into her lap, flicked back the catch, thrust her hand into the large central compartment, and touched metal. Frowning incomprehension, she lifted the thing out. A hissing sound escaped her lips, her hand jerked almost involuntarily, sending a small silvery object arcing through the air to bounce off the coffee table, to roll till half-hidden under the skirt of a chair. A chalice—with a cross and a purple trace of grape juice in its depths.

She sat, heart hammering, hands clenching the purse closed as if to prevent something else escaping. A hard, helpless lump closed her throat. She drew in air pantingly, the effort shaking her thin frame.

"Are you all right?"

She turned her stare from the chalice to the doorway. That woman. She couldn't remember her name. The one Genna had called to stay with her.

Now it was all going to come out. The woman did not look shocked or surprised though, merely a little uncomfortable. Then Ellen realized that she must not be able to see the cup from the doorway.

Go away. Dear God, make her go away.

"Y-yes. I'm fine. Really." She didn't sound fine. Her voice was hoarse, ragged.

Fortunately the woman seemed to be one of those who believed in letting people do their grieving in peace. "Well, if you need anything—" she said, and went back to the kitchen.

As soon as she was gone, Ellen lurched off the sofa, scooped the chalice up, and stuffed it frantically back in the purse.

But what was the use of that? She was no match for the two police officers. Seasoned bloodhounds, they would be able to smell guilt on her. Then, as in some books she had read, bright lights and interminable questions until one would say anything to make it stop. She had learned from Aunt Katherine that it was easier to say what the accuser wanted to hear at the beginning than to make unavailing protestations of innocence.

Please, somebody, tell me what to do.

But they were all against her—all but Genna. And Genna's partisanship had more to do, she was sure, with some perceived duty to Enoch than with any affection for Enoch's cousin. *And if she thinks that I killed him, as she must once she sees this—what will she do?*

Genna looked at the chalice without any particular expression on her face and said, "Where did you get that?"

She had come to replace the other woman just after supper time to find Ellen still at the table, and had sat down opposite. Ellen had produced the cup almost at once from the pocketbook that she'd carried protectively with her most of the afternoon, plunked it down amidst the welter of dirty dishes with a scared but almost defiant, "Here!"

Now, in answer to the question, she said, "It was in my purse."

Genna leaned closer to peer at the cup without touching.

"Did you put it there?"

"I don't know."

The kitchen was silent but for the dripping from the eaves. Genna still looked at the chalice instead of at the other woman, as if it would give her some answer. Finally, without lifting her gaze, she said, "I'm not very good at unselfishness, Ellen. Enoch said it would come with practice, but—" Her shoulders moved. "Frankly, I've been putting my head on the chopping block for you because I owe the Reverend and because"—she turned a palm up—"I do need the practice. Not to mention that provoking the lieutenant was easy enough to be irresistible. But I'm not going to be a martyr for a murderer."

She looked up finally. "So *did* you?" she asked.

"I don't know," Ellen whispered. "I've been over it and over it. Sometimes, it seems I can almost remember—" She stopped and looked down at her twisting hands. "I don't know," she repeated in a resigned tone. "Maybe I should just tell them—"

"Tell them what?" Genna demanded. "That you did it? *How* did you do it then?"

"I don't know. But my mind plays tricks on me sometimes, and I don't remember things. Do you think they would—would understand that?" She looked across at the other with an absurd almost hopeful expression.

"Would they say you were crazy, you mean," Genna said harshly, "and put you in the loony bin instead of prison? Probably. But I don't believe that you're crazy. Enoch said the only thing wrong with your mind was that you'd never been allowed to use it. And that you'd been tricked into believing yourself guilty for a lot of things you never did. I don't think you have the gumption for murder myself. But you almost *want* to believe it, don't you?"

Ellen gaped at her.

"Then you could go into a nice little institution where they'd tell you what to do all the time, just like your aunt did. You'd like that, wouldn't you? Then you'd never have to get any gumption. Well, I should tell you what Enoch told me once. He said, 'I'm not going to make your decisions for you. That's between you and God.' So, go ahead. Confess if you want. Lie your little heart out for a bit of guaranteed security. But don't try to make *me* responsible for it!"

The other woman's expression was like that of a wounded puppy.

"All right, all right!" Genna sighed, snatching up the chalice and beginning to rub at it with a napkin. "I was never very good at this confrontation thing either. It's probably why all my animals are so spoiled. Get me a pair of gloves. I hope you realize this makes me an accessory after the fact, and *I* can't plead insanity."

Ellen was walking on a carpeted floor; her feet made no sound. There were other people in the room with her. She could hear voices at a little distance, but she was detached from them, cloaked in a mantle of invisibility. The mantle was like a fog around her, and she groped through it to find a cloth, pushed the cloth aside till her fingertips touched metal, lifted a lid that was strangely weightless in her hand.

She extended her other hand, and the fog shifted, swirled, writhed, parted suddenly to reveal her fingers poised, stirring something purple in a chalice. White grains trickled like sand from her fingertips into the liquid so that it boiled fiercely and leapt at her as the cup tilted, splashing her with red. The voices in the background rose to a furious shriek.

She came to sitting up in bed with her right wrist soaked. A glass of water she had left on the bedside table had upset over her flailing arm and now lay on the rug.

She must have cried out at some point, because she heard springs squeak in the room across the hall and feet hitting the floor, and Genna appeared in the doorway wearing yards of impossibly flounced white flannel that made her look like a dark and disheveled and cross little angel. Grimm trailed curiously in her wake.

"I had a nightmare," Ellen faltered in explanation, wiping her hand on her blankets. "I dreamed I was dropping poison in the chalice."

"So what?" Genna said, plopping down on the foot

of the bed, arms crossed. "I dreamed I was having a torrid affair with Adam Cullen. That doesn't make it true."

Temporarily distracted, Ellen blinked at her. "Really? With *Adam*?" Then, at a certain gleam in the other's eye, "You're making that up!"

"So?" Genna said. "I was just making a point. Actually it was something totally monotonous about setting out plants. Millions of them." She glowered broodingly at her reflection in the dresser mirror. "According to tradition," she said, "spinsters are supposed to have verr-ry interesting dreams. So how come I get left out?"

"Well, perhaps it *means* something interesting," Ellen comforted.

"It means," Genna said with a sigh, "that I should have set out those perennials two weeks ago."

Greatly daring, Ellen murmured, "Well, I'm sure it means something that it was Adam's name you thought of in connection with torrid affairs."

Genna whirled around to glare outrage, suddenly began to laugh instead. Ellen found herself irresistibly joining in. They laughed until they were weak with it, with more than a hint of hysteria. Perched on top of the dresser, Grimm viewed this display with haughty disapproval.

Finally, wiping tears from her eyes with one of her flounces, Genna said, "Enoch's hardly gone, and *you* start in on me."

"Why?" Ellen asked curiously. "Did Enoch say something about you and Adam too?"

"Never mind," Genna retorted. "It was bad enough that he thought I owed Adam an apology over the garden club farce. Then he had to add insult to injury by saying, well, like I said, never mind—"

But mention of Enoch's name had subdued their high spirits, sent Ellen's mind veering back to her own dream. She shivered, pulled the covers high over her shoulders. "Then you don't think it means anything that I—"

"No, I don't," Genna broke in rather rudely. Actually, here, in the dead of night, it seemed chillingly possible that the woman with the bewildered child's face might be guilty. *How much do I know about psychology, about insanity, after all? Most of the others think it was her. And I take her part because I'm a bit soft-headed, and more than a little naive. Naive enough to rub the fingerprints from a murder instrument and replace that instrument in the soft darkness of an empty church, shoving it far back on a shelf behind old hymnals. Giving my little game with the police high stakes and no way out. I'm getting cold feet,* she thought, and automatically tucked the offending members up under the hem of her gown.

She avoided looking at Ellen until she noticed, from the corner of her eye, that the other woman was staring steadfastly at the bedclothes, *As if afraid*, Genna thought, *of seeing the same evasiveness in me as in the others.*

"I think we better have a wake," Genna said.

Ellen was startled enough to stare across at her again.

"A *wake*?"

"Enoch always said that the attempt to evade reality was responsible for nine tenths of the problems in the world. So we avoid talking about him because it reminds us of how he died, and the fact that he is dead, and that we're going to have to somehow get through this on our own. He wouldn't have liked the fact that we had to stop laughing when we thought of him. So we're going to look things in the eye. I'll go downstairs and get us some food; every wake needs food. Then we're going to stuff ourselves and talk about Enoch and laugh at his jokes, and maybe even cry a little until we realize that the only way he can help us now is through the God he pointed us towards often enough. And then we're going to talk about murder, and the possibility that one of us might get arrested for it. In other words, we're going to think about the worst thing that could possibly happen, and then we're going to say, 'So what?' Okay?"

"Okay," Ellen said meekly.

Late the next afternoon, Genna crawled out of the back seat of Meredith DeWitt's car and stood, leaning on the door for a moment looking in a blank, exhausted sort of way at Adam Cullen, who was sitting with his back against her corral—her broken corral. He had her horse, Gratis, on a rope halter beside him. *Not today,* she thought. *Please, God, I can't take this today.*

She and Ellen had sat up talking almost until dawn. It had done them both some good. Ellen was calmer now, had even asserted her willingness to stay by herself. "I'll have to get used to it sometime," she'd said.

They had just dropped her off at the parsonage, Meredith having driven them into town in the morning to make the funeral arrangements. *It was a good thing we had Meredith along,* Genna thought, *neither of us being exactly the decisive sort.* Meredith had been decisive left and right, choosing everything from the casket to the restaurant where they ate lunch. The other two had been content to trail drowsily in her wake.

But even Meredith isn't going to get me out of this one, Genna thought, exchanging glances with the other woman over the top of the car.

Adam heaved himself upright, looking even larger and more intimidating than usual, and stalked towards them, the horse plodding behind. He ignored Meredith completely. His eyes were narrow, as if hooded against a sun that wasn't shining, his mouth was drawn tight, and something twitched convulsively in one cheek. One look into those eyes, and Genna knew this was the angriest she'd ever seen him. She shrank back a little against the car, hands clutching the door like a shield in front of her.

He stopped, and, swinging the end of the lead rope like a pendulum, said, "Do you know where this animal was?" His voice was quiet, but that was not reassuring.

She tried a pert smile that didn't come off very well.

77

"In one of your fields, I suppose," she said. "I'm sorry if—"

"My fields aren't planted yet," he said tonelessly.

She kept quiet then, waiting.

"This animal," he said, "got into my feed room and did its best to eat itself to death."

She paled, jerked sideways to look at the horse behind him. It seemed a little more subdued than usual, but it raised its head to give her a plaintive whicker.

"It's all right *now*," he said. "Have you ever tried to keep a half-ton animal on its feet when all it wants to do is get down on the floor and tear out its belly with its hooves?"

She shook her head, not it seemed in answer to his question, but in some kind of silent protest, because she continued to shake it as he went on relentlessly.

"That's what I did until the vet got there, and, I can assure you, it is not what you would call an enjoyable experience."

He paused and, hoping he was done, she held out a hand for the lead rope. He ignored it.

"I hear that you don't like the way I farm. Well, after a look at all this, I'd say it's people like yourself who should not be allowed to keep animals. If I had been away somewhere this afternoon, Miss Leon, your horse would have died. And in one of the most agonizing ways possible. I suggest you either get some sense of responsibility or stick to plants!"

"Really, Adam," Meredith said, "I don't think—"

He continued, unheeding, "Now, I'm sure you're going to have some kind of clever comeback to all this, but frankly, I'm not in the mood!" He pitched the end of the rope over Genna's open palm and walked away.

"Really!" Meredith said, and again. *"Really!"*

Genna stepped carefully away from the car, swinging the door shut. "Thank you for your help today, Meredith," she said, "and for the ride."

"Are you all right?" the other asked. "I mean, I can see him being a *little* upset, but really!"

"I'm all right," Genna said and walked away towards the barn, leading the horse.

Meredith turned her car and, wincing at the bumps, drove slowly back out the lane. She braked hard at the junction with Adam's better paved section as a man stepped out in front of her, holding up a hand. Lieutenant Lansky.

He came around to the window. "Do you know where Cullen is?" and, noticing her pale face added, "Anything wrong?"

"I just saw him," she explained, tight-lipped, "and *he's* what's wrong!" She related the scene she had just witnessed. "I mean, I always knew he had a temper, but really—"

"He does seem to have overreacted a little," Lansky agreed cautiously.

"Here he comes now," Rhys said, and the other two

turned their heads to see the farmer taking a shortcut across one of his fields towards the barn.

"Thank you, Mrs. DeWitt," Lansky said, stepping out of her way.

"Something on his mind maybe?" Rhys suggested.

"Something like guilt?" Lansky responded. "Well, let's go see." He had come to find Cullen, because he needed somebody to substantiate the DeWitts' alibi, and Cullen had seemed the most practical and level-headed of the suspects. Had seemed . . .

The whole case was going haywire. The fact that Leona Bentley was his wife's estranged sister might give him a good excuse to hand it over to somebody else. But then, in a rural area like this, almost any cop would be bound to know at least one person who was involved. And it was not like he really knew Leona. The two sisters had quarreled and gone their separate ways before he even met Nancy. He hadn't even remembered her brother-in-law's name. That was who the quarrel had been about, he thought. Nancy hadn't approved of Leona's marriage, and perhaps she had been right about that. There was something wrong in that big house. Leona Bentley was a frightened woman.

Genna put the horse in his boxstall, hung the rope up outside, all with slow, careful movements, as if reluctant to disturb her own numbness—a numbness that, as in a bad wound, would give way to sudden agony. This one, she knew, was going to hurt. And it wouldn't help to know that it was largely due to wounded pride and raw nerves.

For distraction, she thought, *I must remember to return the rope to him. And pay the veterinary bill. How am I going to afford that? Nothing has been selling.*

With any luck, they'll arrest me. They can't make me pay bills when I'm in jail, can they? She started a smile, Gratis poked his head over the top of his stall to give her an affectionate nudge, and her mouth twisted the wrong way and tears coursed down her face, "I'm sorry, Gratis," she whispered. "I'm sorry, Enoch. I'm sorry, God. I should have paid more attention. I should have done better."

Ellen sat in the parsonage living room, pretending to read a book. One part of her brain scanned the words on the page over and over again, but some other part wasn't translating. Was, in fact, concentrating on the darkness, that, even with the curtains drawn, seemed to press against the window panes. A creak somewhere upstairs sent reverberations through her, caused her heartbeat to panic, to lurch and stumble into greater speed. She forced herself to sit still, hands pressing down the pages, and stare towards the door that closed off the foot of the stairs. Was it moving any? She strained her eyes. The white-painted panels seemed to waver, surely . . .

She was being ridiculous. Nobody could have gone upstairs without her seeing them.

It had been quite easy to say that she could stay alone in the unthreatening light of afternoon, but now . . . She stared longingly at the phone. No, she mustn't call Genna. Genna had been bothered enough.

Perhaps I should get a cat. Any other living presence would help.

She looked down at her book again. The sentences had failed to register before, but now one leapt out at her. "Fear is unbelief." Just that simple, harsh, condemning statement. And suddenly she was shakily, fiercely angry.

She threw the book away from her. "As if I could help it!" she whispered to herself, jumping up and beginning to pace. "As if I should *enjoy* myself with a murderer somewhere out there or somewhere inside of me. As if I should be *calm.*"

One phrase beat back into her mind like an echo. *Or somewhere inside of me.* Inside *of me.*

Unable to flee that, she stopped, leaning against a lamp table, her hands spread flat on its surface, staring down at the glowing bulb as if mesmerized.

Because if it were inside her, it couldn't be banished, not with locked doors or drawn curtains or light. No way to get rid of it. Or, perhaps one way.

She laughed a little, chokingly. Oh, yes, there was one way. Not that she'd ever have the nerve for it.

Though it would be a thankful release for everyone concerned. Now she was just an embarrassing nuisance to them all. Dead, she might still be a nuisance, but one that could be dealt with, buried. And they would have an excuse for her. *Poor thing. She didn't know what she was doing. She just wasn't right, is all.*

But her Aunt Katherine had said and others had said . . . the ultimate sin. Chesterton had said that too, and there was no one more opposite her aunt than Chesterton. The big, exuberant Catholic with a child's enthusiasm and lust for life. Her aunt would have hated Chesterton. Yet they had agreed on this one thing. Suicide was sin. Her aunt had insisted on it, Ellen suspected, to keep anyone from *escaping* that way. But why had Chesterton?

She went across to the bookcases, fumbled out a paperback. *Orthodoxy.* Such a stuffy title for such an alive book. Part of his sense of humor, no doubt.

She leafed through the pages till she found the passage, had to concentrate to keep the words from blurring under her gaze. A slap in the face of God. A refusal to take an interest. She shoved the book angrily back. Why *should* she take an interest? God hadn't, had He? All she got from heaven was silence.

She was rather shocked at the irreverence of her own thoughts. She was beginning to sound like Max Rourke. Not that she could disbelieve in God. Her aunt had shoved Him at her for years, and now, free, Ellen found she still couldn't leave Him alone. She sat back down in her chair, shivering. *You wouldn't seek Me, if you hadn't found Me.* The words leapt to sudden life in her brain. No, it wasn't God talking. It was just a quote she'd read somewhere. Or maybe that was the way God talked. Not from the outside, but from the inside.

You wouldn't seek if you hadn't found. Paradox. What did it mean? She leaned forward, frowning, hands clenched together as she strove to follow. That maybe God wasn't someone you located for once and all. That maybe it was the seeking, the constant weary painful groping that was the point. The *caring*. The letting go of smug surety and the willingness to live with constant effort. With risk. What Chesterton would call the adventure.

Why seek ye the living among the dead? Why had that popped in? Her eyes widened. Because, because . . . her thoughts stammered in their haste. Satisfaction was death. Because it was the end; it didn't go anywhere. That was why Christ had railed at the hypocrites, in an attempt to break through to them, to raise them up. Maybe that was why He had made it so hard for them to know who He was. *Don't tell them. They have to find out for themselves. They have to be desperate.*

Desperation was one thing she had plenty of. She smiled blindly down at her clenched hands. Maybe she was getting a sense of humor after all.

She straightened up and looked around her at the

room. It seemed friendlier somehow. What to do now? She felt too restless, her thoughts still too tense—for reading. She must find herself some more hobbies. Knitting perhaps, or gardening. Gardening. She had actually started that. Genna had given her some seeds of perennials to plant, had told her that they grew best in cool weather. *Lucky perennials.* She giggled to herself. She must learn to be a perennial. And she had planted them, rather clumsily, sure that they wouldn't come up because she didn't know what she was doing. Where had she put them? Under the kitchen window.

Without really thinking about it, she went into the kitchen, switched on the light, went out the side door and around to the front. She knelt down to look, and there they stood in the light shining dimly from inside. Green, in rows! Fresh and intense-looking and alive.

She touched them reverently and giggled again, lay down flat on her stomach in the damp grass to look at them more closely. It was ridiculous that a few little plants could make her feel like this. Max would think it impossibly corny. She mentally thumbed her nose at Max Rourke. The man was a wimp. But Chesterton, she thought, would have approved. And so did Somebody Else, if old G.K. was right. She rolled over on her back to look up at a sky full of rushing dark clouds.

And then it hit her. She was outside; she was actually outside in the dangerous dark with the rustling yews and a noise like footsteps And, not only wasn't she scared, she was reveling in it. Lying in wet grass, soaked and cold to the bone, and laughing like a maniac. But she was alive; *dear God, she was finally alive!*

The milk truck pulled into the lane at two o'clock in the morning. The driver had had a breakdown earlier in the day, had had to wait for another truck to be finished and pumped out.

Half-awake, Genna listened to the laboring of the truck's engine up the grade, the shush of its airbrakes as it slowed for the turn. She had taken a hot bath, but even then, it had required a half hour under the blankets to get her warm again.

Genna turned and muttered in restless sleep after the headlights flashed across her window as the truck veered left toward Adam's farm, pulled a blanket over her head. Her cat opened its eyes, growled disapproval of this change in routine.

At the barn, the driver inserted the truck's hose through the requisite hole in the milkhouse wall. It was quiet inside except for the rap of his shoes on cement and the ticking of an electric clock. He lifted one of the round lids off the huge tank to abstract a routine sample, went back out into the windy night to switch on the pump. Inside again, he frowned at the sample. Something that looked like dirt in it. *Strange. Cullen's milk is usually premium grade. Good thing this isn't the day for the bacteria test*

He yawned, began to jot down the usual information on his clipboard. He lifted off a lid again to make sure the pump was doing its job, rubbed his eyes before he peered down into the tank. If they didn't find an extra driver somewhere, he would only be taking this truck back to pick up another and restart his route immediately. The ticking was lulling, like that of the old-fashioned alarm clock he kept beside his bed. He jerked awake, not quite remembering what he was doing, stared fuzzily into the almost empty tank.

Strangely, when he saw the human body close up against the big paddle, his first despairing thought was, *And after all this, they'll have to throw out the whole truckful!* And the ticking of the clock seemed louder and faster in the thick silence.

I am afraid of all my sorrows, I
know that thou wilt not hold me
innocent.
Job 9:28

In an interrogation room at police headquarters, Adam Cullen sat forward in his chair, elbows propped on his thighs, big hands dangling between his knees, and stared at the floor. It was ten o'clock in the morning, and the two police officers had been going at him since six. He had protested again and again that he must get home, that he had cows that needed to be milked, and they had paid little attention. He had long ago stopped answering their questions, questions that always circled back to the murder of his former hired hand and his supposed guilt in the matter.

They had plenty of ammunition. On Monday morning, the milk truck driver had seen the fierce argument that ensued when Lawson abruptly quit his job—the same driver who had knocked on the trailer door at two o'clock Wednesday morning to report his grisly discovery.

The driver had seemed, at first, disposed to see the whole thing as some kind of freak accident, but had grown increasingly edgy as they awaited the arrival of an ambulance and the police, had cast a lot of sidelong glances. It would have had to be a very strange accident.

The police dismissed any question of an accident at once. Someone had hit Lawson hard over the head and heaved the body into the tank, they decided, by means of the long lid that could be lifted up for cleaning. Whether the blow had killed him or he had drowned was yet to be determined. The refrigeration involved tended to make matters a little tricky, but the police surgeon was pretty sure that the man had been dead by eleven the previous evening. Lawson had boarded with an elderly couple in the village. Wakened at dawn, they had given a groggy statement to the effect that their boarder had left the house shortly before nine—on foot—without volunteering his destination.

As for the crime itself, almost anyone could have done it—even a woman. Lawson had been a small man, and the tank wasn't that high. The police seemed little inclined, though, to look further than the hand's big, burly ex-employer who was known to possess a tricky temper and a strong grievance against the deceased. And who else would Lawson have come to the farm to see?

They kept coming back to Adam, and he had altogether given up trying to answer them. The whole thing was just so unexpected, so preposterous that he could still hardly believe in its reality. Outside it was raining again. The fields were already so soft, this would put off spring planting another week at least. If he were permitted to do any planting. That was when it really hit him, like a fist to the stomach. He could go to prison for this; men had been convicted on less evidence. To a jury, it would all seem so obvious.

Head down, he ignored Lansky's insistent voice. Foster had warned him once. "Your philosophy seems to run along the lines of heaven helps those who help themselves," the minister had said, "and I'd like to remind you that that isn't Scripture. Someday you're not going to be able to help yourself."

It seemed that day had come. And who else would have any inclination to help him? Foster would have, but Foster was dead. The other suspects would be only too happy to have the heat off of them. The other farmers had never liked him anyway; they would feel vindicated.

It seemed suddenly important that he find someone

somewhere who would care what happened to him. His mind scrambled over the names of those he might consider friends and neighbors and found no reassurance.

Lansky was talking about Foster now. Adam looked glassily at him, and away again. The sergeant had been silent for a while. Maybe he wasn't quite as sure as his superior was, or maybe it was just some version of good cop, bad cop. They would try to fob Foster's murder off on him too, because who would believe two different murderers in a tiny community like his.

Someone called Rhys to the phone, and he went away, but Lansky kept on. Adam supposed it was a wearing away process like water on stone. In fact, there was a leak somewhere, and a constant drip-drip that was almost as bad as the lieutenant's voice.

Lansky had started out with a wheedling persuasiveness, but switched eventually to a harsh almost-yell as if trying to snap Cullen out of his lethargy. The suspect didn't respond except to repeat, at intervals, that their detaining him was making animals suffer. Rhys came back and remained silent as the day dragged on.

Someone rapped at the door, and everyone in the room seemed relieved at the interruption. Adam even lifted his stoic gaze. "There's a woman out here who wants to make a statement about the case," an officer said "A Miss Leon?"

Lansky turned a triumphant gaze on his prisoner

"Send her in." She probably just wanted to report on Cullen's temper the previous afternoon, but she might have an effect on his silence too. Already, he was visibly wilting.

Genna was, the farmer thought, the least likely of his acquaintances to be sympathetic, and who could blame her for that? He had grossly overreacted to the horse thing. She had, after all, been busy the last couple days looking after Ellen Foster. She had also just lost one of her closest friends. He had known, even as the caustic words spewed out, that he was going to regret them, but had somehow lacked the willpower to stop that venting of frustration and exhaustion. It was not just having to do all that milking alone either. Perhaps Foster's death had hit him harder than he'd realized, had, for some reason, left him with a niggling doubt, a dissatisfaction.

A bellow from outside made them all jump. "Hey, you can't take that animal in there. Here, stop!" And Genna Leon was in the room, but not alone. Something that had been walking close to her leg, partially obscured by her long full skirts, now bolted free, launched itself across the room and up against Adam's chair. After one brief, licking lunge at his face, the black and white collie dropped down onto its stomach next to his boots.

Completely ignoring the officer who loped in frantically after her, Genna pulled out a chair from the table, sat down on it, and arranged her skirts primly. The dog growled

Lansky said, "Okay, Blaine. Leave it." But he was beginning to look a little uneasy.

Genna looked pale, and there were dark circles under her eyes. The fluorescent light was not kind, and she appeared less pixieish than usual. She sat with her hands neatly folded in her lap and said, "Good morning, gentlemen. I've come to give your chief suspect here an alibi."

They all looked dumbfounded, including the chief suspect.

"Are you implying," Lansky managed finally, "that you were *with* Cullen last night?"

Genna frowned. "Of course not. You've got to get that mind out of the gutter, Lieutenant. But I know where he was during the important hours—nine to eleven, wasn't it?"

"And just how do you know what the important hours are, Miss Leon?" the lieutenant inquired dangerously.

"I got it from your sergeant," she said. "Didn't he tell you?"

Lansky turned to look at Rhys, who became immediately preoccupied with his own fingernails.

"But I suppose I should start at the beginning," Genna continued, "with the big scene about my horse."

"We know all about that," the lieutenant said.

"Good." Genna smoothed her skirt. She hadn't looked in Adam's direction since her entrance "It was rather . . . painful, and I'd just as soon not go into it anyway. Well, over supper that evening, I decided I had really better go and apologize."

They all swiveled round to stare at her. "Apologize?" Lansky and Rhys chorused together.

"Of course. I mean, he was right, you know. Because of my irresponsibility, Gratis could have died. In fact, I think some people would have just let him die to teach me a lesson. So when God told me—"

"God?" Lanksy choked. He was sitting down now with one hand over his face. "What does God have to do with this?"

"Well, you don't think the apologizing idea was mine, do you?" Genna flared. "At the time, I felt more like slashing the man's tires. Or his throat. But God is kind of relentless on this truth thing. So I argued with Him about it for a while. Then I started up the lane as slow as I could go, fighting all the while. This was around eight-thirty. The light was on in Adam's trailer, and I saw him in there hunched over the computer. I lost my nerve completely. It started to drizzle a bit, and I stood out there getting chilled to the bone, and telling God to give me a minute or two to think up something to say. Well, those minutes kind of stretched. I even tried the one about how it wouldn't look too good, my going to see him that time of night, but I don't think God was impressed. He doesn't worry too much about how things look, you know."

His lieutenant being speechless, Rhys put in an encouraging, "No?"

"No," she said glumly. "He has this obsession with how things really are. Anyway, I left it too long, because the light went off eventually, and I said, 'See, he's gone to bed; I'll come back tomorrow.' It was close on midnight when I got home."

A short silence ensued. Rhys looked at Lansky. Cullen leaned back in his chair, his hand on his dog's ruff. He appeared wary and bewildered.

"Do you mean to tell me, Miss Leon," Lansky said, voice muffled, "that you stood out there in the rain for over three hours?"

"It seemed much longer," she said.

"Putting you," he continued, "right at the scene of the crime while it was happening?"

"Well, not right at," she said. "The milkhouse is on the other end of the barn. I couldn't see it from where I was."

"But you could have walked around the barn," Lansky pursued, "and gone into the milkhouse and hit Lawson over the head and dumped him in the milk tank?"

"And why would I do a thing like that?"

"Because he saw you pick up the chalice on Sunday maybe. Because you knew Cullen was on bad terms with him and would probably get blamed for the whole thing."

"And then I come down and give him an alibi that puts me right on the spot?"

Lansky slammed out of his chair and went to stand with his back to them, looking out the window.

"And just when was it that Sergeant Rhys here was so helpful about all this?" he asked.

"Oh, that was this morning. I kept getting an impression of lights and voices all night, but thought I was dreaming. I woke up early and knew Adam would be doing his milking, so I decided to get the whole thing over with. But scarcely had I got to the top of my lane than I saw you taking him away in a police car. So I went back home to get myself some breakfast and think that one over. Then all the cows started to bawl and Shep started to bark. After I'd listened to that long enough to get a screaming headache, I called up the police station to see what was going on. I asked for the sergeant because I thought he might be a little more reasonable about telling me, and he was. So then I saw I would have to come down here—I drove your truck, Adam, by the way—but first I called up Ben Grover to do something about the cows."

At Adam's involuntary movement of protest, she said, "He might not be very fond of you, but he could hardly refuse to help out under the circumstances. I mean, Christian charity and suffering animals and all that. I must admit that I laid it on rather thick, but he finally said he'd come. Since your milkhouse is sealed off and thus the pipeline too, he said he'd bring some old milking machines over and borrow a truckload of cans from some Amish guy he knows. But he's not going to be able to do it all alone, so—" She half-rose. "I assume we're free to go now?"

Lansky didn't turn or answer. Rhys said cautiously, "I guess so. Just don't leave the state—either of you."

Genna quelled an irritable impulse to snap, "Oh, dear, there goes my spring jaunt to Paris!"

From his position at the window, Lansky watched them walk through the rain to a truck in the parking lot. The dog seemed the only happy one, half-prancing with ears and tail alert.

Damp and exhausted, Genna sat bolt-upright in the passenger seat with her hands clenched in her lap. An uncomfortable silence ensued as Adam swung the truck, water hissing under the tires, onto the blacktop. The wipers beat a steady monotone. Looking straight ahead through the streaming windshield, Genna finally took a deep breath and plunged. "I want to say that I'm sorry about Gratis—"

"There's no need—" Adam started to interrupt. She lurched forward, putting her hands on the dashboard, and glared at him around the dog.

"It took me long enough to get up the nerve for this," she gritted, "and you are going to listen to it!"

Then she sat back, looked forward again, and started over, talking rapidly as if to prevent further interjection.

"I want to say that I'm sorry about the trouble Gratis caused you. I knew that corral was in bad shape, and I should have attended to it. And I want to thank you for making so much effort to save him. It was really more than I deserved, and I am grateful. You can send me the bill from the vet and tell me how much of your feed Gratis ate, and I'll pay for that too."

When he remained silent, she finally peeked at him around the dog's head. "Okay?"

Steady gaze on the road, he said, "I already paid the vet."

"Well, you can tell me how much it—"

"No."

Close to tears, she flared at him, "Why? So you can feel martyred and virtuous about the whole thing? I—"

"So," he interrupted, "I can pay a little bit for the brutal things I said. You didn't make excuses for yourself, so I won't either. In any case, the way I acted was inexcusable. I'm sorry." After this stiff little speech, he looked at her finally. "Okay?"

"Okay," she said in a small, surprised voice.

"You have a bad effect on me," he said dryly, attention back on his driving.

"On the lieutenant too," she said, leaning against the door and following a raindrop with her finger against the glass. "So I don't fit very well into your comfortable little worlds. I'm a little too extreme for you all maybe, but I never thought religion was supposed to be a hobby that you pick up only when you feel like it." She blinked. "Now I'm being self-righteous, aren't I? Sorry." She tilted back her head, switched her gaze in his direction. The dog lay on the seat, and she found that Adam was looking at her again without any particular expression.

"In a world where people worry more about dolphin than human babies, some of us had better go a little crazy," she finished, and closed her eyes.

They rode in silence for a few minutes. "How am I supposed to pay Grover back for this?" he asked then.

She bounced upright on the seat, said, "See, that! That attitude is exactly why nobody likes you!" Then she paused, appalled at herself.

A slight smile twitched his lips. "Thanks," he said.

"No," she flustered. "No, I didn't mean that precisely. Yes, I did," she decided suddenly, plowing ahead. "You have to be so self-sufficient. I mean, you can go all charitable yourself, when you feel like it, but you won't allow anything in return. That's why you insisted on playing superman and milking your great horde of cows yourself after Lawson walked out when it would have been only common decency to ask for help. What you should do is ask Ben for another favor while you're at it."

She flopped back. "Sorry," she muttered again.

"What do you know about that chalice?" he asked, looking at her profile.

Not so much as a quiver of an eyelash betrayed her. She continued her bleary survey of the passing scenery.

Her hands remained loose in her lap. Her "What do you mean?" was a triumph of disinterested casualty, but it was too disinterested.

"Your face," he said. "When Lansky mentioned the cup, you got that dangerously innocent expression of yours. I've seen it before, don't forget."

They were pulling into the lane. She stretched, looked at him squarely. "Are you sure you're not imagining things?"

As he braked in front of the barn, he said, "Meaning to deceive is the same thing as lying, you know."

The rain had stopped. The sun came out, diffusing the mist that hovered over the muddy ground. Climbing out of the truck, she said, "You don't need any more help, do you?"

"Sure do," he said. "Come along. Ben and I can run the milkers, but somebody's going to have to pour all that milk into the cans."

She looked at him without enthusiasm. "I was just being polite."

"I know," he said, a certain glint in his eye, "but you're the one who said I should ask for help when I need it."

"Me and my big mouth," she muttered as she followed him into the barn.

"Hi, Ben," Adam said in a casual tone. "Thanks for coming."

He got a surly grunt in reply from the older man, who was tossing a wide belt over a cow's back. Adam picked up one of the machines himself, started to turn away, hesitated. "If you don't mind, there's something I'd like to ask your advice about later."

Grover, hunkered down now, attaching the suction cups to the cows udder, gave him a quick, startled glance, then turned his attention back to the his work. His mumbled reply seemed, though, to be in the affirmative.

Later, stepping down into the aisle for the umpteenth time to slosh frothy white liquid from a machine into buckets, Adam glanced up towards the rows of milk cans to see how Genna was getting along. The barn cats had been following her up and down, getting underfoot, and, the last time he'd seen her, she'd been carrying a bucket in one hand and a bunch of kittens in her skirt. Now he saw that she had upended one of the milk can lids to make a saucer for the cats. The kittens, though, kept getting crowded out. As he watched, she dipped a hand into her bucket, brought it out with a palmful of milk which she held down to a kitten's level. Her tense expression lightening, she laughed as its rough tongue tickled her hand, then she reached back in the bucket for more as the other kittens rushed her.

Grover stepped down into the aisle too, took in the scene. The two men exchanged glances, and grins.

"Watch it, kid," Ben said. "She'll start to grow on you."

Late that afternoon, Genna was setting out perennial seedlings in her garden. Her lack of sleep the night before and the labor of the morning was beginning to tell on her. Her eyes felt dry, grainy, her muscles flaccid. The ground was really too soggy for planting. It was also cold. She rubbed her eyes with the back of a muddy hand.

"You look frightful," a young voice said over her head.

She looked up. Tanya Bentley in a rabbit fur jacket and high-heeled boots stood critically regarding her. "You have mud all over your face and humongous bags under your eyes," the teenager said. "Don't you care how you look?"

"The mud would be an improvement over the paint you're wearing," Genna came back sourly. "Don't *you* care that you look like a slut?"

Seeming unperturbed, Tanya said, "Maybe I am one."

"Then why aren't you out on a street corner somewhere instead of here aggravating me?"

Head cocked to one side, Tanya considered that, and laughed. The humor did not match the harsh lines of strain under the makeup.

"I'm taking a walk," she said. "The country gentleman's daughter. All I need is an Irish Setter."

"Don't forget the tweed jacket," Genna said, jamming another delphinium in place.

"Come to ask the local white witch for some advice," Tanya pursued, pacing up and down behind the other woman.

"Good-oh," Genna said. "Do you want your palm read, or shall I take a peek at my crystal ball?"

"What kind of attitude is that?" Tanya asked. "Aren't you religious types supposed to encourage troubled youth to confide in you and all that?"

"You youths aren't the only ones with troubles," Genna said, slicing between seedlings in the flat with a sharp knife. "But, I suppose if it's my duty and all— Go ahead, confide. Are you pregnant?"

"I'm not that stupid," the other drawled.

"I never thought you were," Genna said. "In fact, I suspect you of being quite shrewd, and quite chaste too. Am I right?"

At the other's startled questioning look, she said, "The clothes and the attitude. Overdone, you know."

Tanya laughed again, nervously, sat down on a rock, and shoved her hands into her pockets.

"No guy is going to ruin my life," she said venomously.

"So it's a guy."

"Kind of." Tanya stared off at the gray horizon, dug one heel into the ground, brought the words out in an abrupt nervous rush, "My father hits my mother "

The knife in Genna's hand slipped, cutting a fuzzy silver lychnis plant neatly in two. Kneeling there, staring blindly down at the flat, she said in her mind, *No, God, I don't want to hear this. Make her be joking.*

She looked up finally. Tanya was still looking resolutely into the distance. She looked impossibly young and scared, like a little girl dressed up in grown-up clothes. She wasn't joking.

Wearily, Genna set the flat aside. "So what are we going to do about it?" she asked.

Tanya's head jerked around. "You believe me?"

"I don't see any reason why you should lie about it. How long has this been going on?"

"For years. It's gotten worse lately though. It used to be just once in a while. Now it's almost every day."

Genna felt sick. For years. For years Leona Bentley had been acting like a scared rabbit, holed up in that big house of hers, canceling appointments at the last minute, always giggling nervously about her accident-proneness. When she did venture out, always a cringing eager-to-please attitude, an overdone gratitude for the smallest favors. *And none of us saw it. None of us cared enough to see it.*

"Does he hit you too?" she asked.

"Once," Tanya said. "When I was twelve. I broke a lamp over his head. I told him that if he ever touched me again I would kill him. And I meant it." Her lip curled scornfully. "He's a coward really. But mother's just too weak to stand up to him "

She pulled up some grass to rub mud off one boot heel. "It isn't just the beating. He puts down every single thing she does. How else can you expect her to be?" she demanded defiantly.

"Does she drink?"

"Some. Not as much as everybody thinks. It doesn't seem to help her any. She would rather have people think she's a sot than—that. She's terrified of anybody finding out."

You were too, Genna thought, *before you started growing up.* For all their defiance and rebellion, teens are more terrified than adults of being talked about by their peers, of being different.

"Your mother will be at the funeral tomorrow, won't she?"

"Yeah."

"I'll talk to her afterwards—at the parsonage. Perhaps if she knows that somebody else knows, she won't have any reason for hiding anymore."

Tanya looked skeptical, but relieved, as if something being done was better than nothing. "Okay." She lurched awkwardly up. "Well, thanks—and everything, you know."

"I know Tanya—" Genna hesitated, plunged on "You don't think Enoch might have found out and—"

"And one of them killed him because of it?" Tanya asked bluntly. "I think he was figuring it out. He was my Great White Hope there for a while. And I just don't know How can I?"

"Go see Ellen," Genna said suddenly. "And tell her about everything."

"The mouse?" Tanya asked, startled. "Why?"

"Because the mouse, as you call her, has been through a lot of the same sort of thing you and your mother have. Not so much of the physical abuse as the mental part. I can't pretend to understand something I haven't experienced. But she can, and she needs to get it out of her system as much as you do."

"Maybe," Tanya muttered, turning away. "I'm not much for the spilling of guts thing. And she doesn't like me."

"She doesn't really *know* you," Genna said. "Frankly, I'm beginning to think that none of us supposed brothers and sisters in Christ know each other at all." She stabbed her trowel into the dirt. "We're too good at pretending things are fine. Maybe that means we don't know Him at all either."

CHAPTER 6

**And it came to pass, when they
had brought them forth abroad,
that he said, Escape for thy
life; look not behind thee, neither stay thou in all the plain;
escape to the mountain, lest
thou be consumed.**
Genesis 19:17

G enna was restless that night. She paced and could
not settle into anything. The books and magazines she tried to peruse seemed banal, irrelevant.

A danger signal was blinking in her mind with the
mesmerizing tendency of a red strobe light. She was
getting in too deep everywhere. She had been a withdrawn, extremely careful child. And, though in adult-
hood she had rebelled against her youth by her unusual
dress and lifestyle, more of that attitude remained than
had been erased. It kept her emotionally detached.

The eyes of Enoch's portrait seemed to follow her around the room. Perhaps that was why Tanya had come to her, because that detachment could be misread as levelheadedness. Or because Tanya herself wanted a detached sort of judgment on the matter—no slobbering.

Irritably, she thought that she understood now why people smoked. It gave them something to do with their hands. She went to the portrait, daubed at it with a brush. But it was done; further fiddling would probably ruin it.

She moved back a distance, glared at it hazily. Hers was not a peculiar attitude for artistic types. Most artists she'd known had it to one degree or another. It was almost a necessity when your job was social commentary. To make judgments on the world almost implied one's separation from it. Perhaps that was why judging was forbidden at the same time that separation was demanded. Her vision clearing, she glowered at Enoch Foster's smiling face. She wanted to whine that it didn't make sense. And could almost hear his relentless reply, "If you can't accept paradox, you can't accept Christianity."

Perhaps Max's opinion of her was true after all. She wanted the sentimental trappings—the consolation—of religion without allowing it to disturb her comfort. And there rang through her mind as loudly as if it had been spoken beside her the final words on that: "White tombs full of dead bones. Generation of vipers!"

She started violently, looked around her at the bright room, empty of all other life. Even Grimm was absent, off on an evening prowl.

She didn't generally get lonely, but any distraction would be welcome now.

Frankly, she didn't want to get tangled up in the lives of a neurotic woman or a disturbed teenager or a battered wife. Or especially—her gaze veered in the direction of Adam's farm—of a man whose sudden flashes of humor and perceptiveness had rather messed up her neat little category for him.

She had been herded into this choice, she thought bitterly, and had gone easily, straight down the chute of her own egotistical dispensing of free advice—only realizing too late where it would end up. And now there was only yes or no, because refusing to choose was a choice in itself, and it usually meant no.

It would be easy to evade, go away and visit her family for a month or two. Fatally easy.

The next morning Genna and Ellen sat in the parsonage kitchen and waited for the DeWitts to pick them up for the funeral. "Tanya came to see me last night," Ellen said.

Genna looked up. "Did she tell you?"

"Yes." Ellen stared out the window. "She was quite unemotional about it. She wanted to hear how I'd coped. When I told her about it all, she actually wept. I think that's strange, don't you? She wouldn't cry for herself, but she cried for me."

Shielding her eyes from a sudden sunlight, she said, "I was never very comfortable around her. Around any teenagers. They're always so, so—"

"Boisterous?" Genna suggested. "They feel more than older people, I think. Maybe that's why none of us would really want to go back. We've learned to tone things down—or tune them out."

"She wasn't at all," Ellen said, "like I thought she was. It's made me wonder how many other people I've been wrong about. It even made me wonder a little about my aunt—about what kind of childhood she might have had, and—and things."

"Enoch would be proud of you," Genna said. The sun came out full and shone across the table at which they sat. She was fiddling with the sugar spoon again, and she tipped crystals from it to watch them fall through the light.

The funeral was not as bad as she had expected. "None of that dirgelike music for me," Enoch had said once. "Keep it brief—and smile!" And they did smile— through tears—as they sang "Amazing Grace" *a cappella*. The sun blazed through the stained glass windows and glittered in the gemlike waterdrops beading the daffodils outside as the coffin was carried from the church to the graveyard behind it.

Afterwards, the parsonage was crowded and confused with women carrying in covered dishes around knots of black-coated men. Genna was frantically searching for serving spoons when the Bentleys came in. Leona, looking even sicker than usual, was half-supported by her husband. "We shouldn't stay too long," Elliot was explaining apologetically to somebody. "The wife's not feeling well." Genna's gaze met Tanya's across the room.

"She looks like she's going to throw up," the teenager said abruptly. "She'd better go in the bathroom," and dragged her mother away.

Genna drifted around the table, nodding and saying hello's, sticking spoons in pasta salads and pots of baked beans. She eased her way out of the kitchen and around the corner to the bathroom, rapped softly on the door.

Tanya was waiting for her and opened the door enough to let her wiggle through. Leona was sitting on the closed toilet, staring apathetically at nothing. "She's taken some of her tranquilizers," the teenager said. "It helps her get away from things.

"She worked all yesterday afternoon on some cheese puffs to bring here. Then *he* came home, said they were trash, and threw them out. I'm going to kill him, Genna," she added in the same expressionless tone, "I'm really going to kill him."

Leona didn't seem to hear anything that was said. She merely sat, quite still, like a wax mannequin with the same blank eyes.

Genna fumbled with the cross around her neck, said, "All right. We'll get her out. Today."

"How?" the teenager asked flatly. "He has the keys to the car. And where?"

"Her sister," Genna said. "Lieutenant Lansky's wife."

"They haven't spoken to each other for years."

"I don't see how she could refuse," Genna said vaguely. "Being a cop's wife. In an emergency." She was thinking about cars. Hers certainly wouldn't do; it overheated on the slightest provocation and had to be nursed along. And Enoch's, the one that now belonged to Ellen, would be in the garage, blocked in by those of the guests. She went across to look out the window at the driveway. Then, "Stay here," she said. "Lock the door. I'll be back in a minute."

She went into the living room and located Adam by the fireplace, talking to Garth DeWitt. Someone grabbed her arm, inquiring about coffee filters. "Ask Ellen," she said, then wove her way through the crowd. "Could I speak to Adam for a minute?" she said bluntly to DeWitt. He raised his eyebrows, flashed a knowing grin. "Sure, sure," he said, backing off in an exaggerated manner.

"Out here," she said to Adam, leading him across to the door that opened out on the backyard. Heads turned curiously to watch them.

The sun had gone in; the air was chilly. Rubbing at her forearms nervously, she told the farmer about

114

Leona. He listened without comment. "So," she finished, "can we borrow your truck?"

Here, Cullen thought, was the sticking point. Here was where he should back off, decline to get involved. If the woman had wanted to leave, he should point out logically, she could have done so long ago. It was really none of his affair. These domestic matters could be tricky, with the wife often turning on those who had thought to rescue her. There might even be charges of kidnapping. It could get very messy. Then why was he already reaching in his pocket for his keys?

For the briefest instant, his mind looked wistfully back on how peaceful his life had been up to this point, and his fingers hesitated. Then he thought how unpeaceful Leona's had been, maybe because others like him had that little motto about minding one's own business.

He plucked the keys out and dropped them in Genna's outstretched palm. "Do you want me to go along?" he asked.

"There won't be room," she said, "but thanks. If you need to go anywhere, you can use my car." A rueful half-smile quivered on her lips. "It takes about a gallon of water per mile. The radiator leaks." She started to turn back inside. His voice stopped her with her hand on the knob.

"What if her sister won't take her?"

Genna shrugged, spread her hands. "I don't know. A hotel maybe? We'll find something."

"Just a minute." He pulled a blue vinyl folder from the inner pocket of his jacket, scribbled his signature at the bottom of a blank check, ripped it off and held it out to her. "You can cash that at the bank in town. Put them on a plane to somewhere if you have to."

Max Rourke started out the door behind them just then, viewed this transaction with pursed lips and one lifted brow, and started to say something. But Genna saw, over the shoulders of people in between, Elliot Bentley leaving the kitchen and heading for the bathroom door. "Max!" she said, grabbing his arm and shoving. "Quick! Go get Elliot away from there! Hurry!"

"Whatever," Rourke muttered to himself, pushing rudely through a group in his path. "Hey, Bentley!" he raised his voice. "Wanta talk to you!"

He found Adam right behind him. "Both of us want to talk to you," Adam said, putting a hand on Elliot's arm. "Privately." He tugged the older man gently toward the back door. "We've both got some extra money that needs investing and need some advice." He cast a warning glance at Rourke over Bentley's head.

Why all this theater to keep the poor guy from going to the bathroom? Max wondered. *It's kind of entertaining anyway. Something to get my mind off things.* His mind always needed distractions after a funeral. The words of an old song spun through his thoughts. "Stop the world and let me off. I'm tired of going round and round." Round and round about covered it.

Ellen had been trapped in one corner of the living room by those offering comfort. She occasionally got a brief peek at what was going on: Genna leading Adam away, then Adam and Max leading Elliot away. Now Genna was sidling back towards the bathroom.

Meredith DeWitt was sitting beside Ellen on the couch, talking in a bracing, no-nonsense manner. *This,* Ellen supposed, *is to keep me from making a spectacle of myself with grief.* Not that she had time for grieving anyway, what with worry about the living. Enoch, she realized, would have wanted it that way.

Meredith, she noticed suddenly, was following the direction of her gaze. Ellen quickly snapped her own attention back and tried to think of something distracting to say. "I love your necklace." A simple gold choker. "I like that red and black one you have too. The beads, you know. They would have gone good with that outfit. What is it you call them? Rosary peas, was it?"

Meredith was looking at her strangely. *Oh, no, I've insulted her. I didn't mean—* "Of course, that one looks fine with it too," she babbled on. "Lovely." Why did she sound so unconvincing? "I suppose the other one wouldn't have been appropriate anyway."

Get off this subject somehow, stupid, she told herself. *You know nothing about jewelry anyhow.* She cast a surreptitious glance towards the bathroom. The door was now standing open. All these jitters were making Meredith suspicious.

Why shouldn't Meredith know anyway? Because, for one thing, Meredith had never liked Leona. Ellen fumbled for a new subject. Her gaze lit on a bouquet someone had brought from the church. Flowers. Of course! "Your arrangement of tulips was lovely Sunday," she said. "It must have taken you forever—" She stopped. Could that be an insult too? "Or maybe they just looked like they took a long time?" she concluded weakly. "Did they?" *Somebody,* she prayed, *get me out of this.*

Outside, Genna and Tanya had to half lift Leona onto the high seat of the truck, her heels scrabbling on the running board. Tanya climbed in beside her, and Genna hurried around to the driver's side. They had made it through the kitchen with Genna muttering a breezy something about taking Leona home. "Don't tell Daddy," Tanya had said to the women there. "He'll just worry."

They had got some strange looks though. Either people knew something was going on, or they were just plain edgy, or maybe a little of both.

Genna hiked her own narrow skirt up over her knees so she could get her leg up, got a grip on the steering wheel to give herself a boost. *Why must they make trucks so high, anyway?* Something to do with four-wheel drive and roughing it and bouncing over three foot rocks in advertisements, she supposed.

Tanya had found a pad of paper on the dashboard,

was scribbling something on it. "Just a minute," she said, jumped down from the seat, and ran to stick the note under a wiper on her father's car. As she vaulted breathlessly back into the seat beside her mother, slammed the door, Genna turned the key and said, "I hope you didn't tell him where we were going."

"Not a chance!" Tanya said. "I told him not to bother looking for us because we were never coming back."

The engine turned over beautifully and started at once. Not used to this cooperativeness on the part of engines, it took Genna a moment to react. Then she saw the door of the house start to open, whipped the vehicle into reverse, and shot it backwards down the driveway. She made a sudden swerve to miss the mailbox, then was on the road, barely touching the brake before slamming into drive and hitting the gas. Thrown over against her mother, Tanya giggled, picked herself up, and continued to giggle with a kind of crazy delight as the house receded into the distance behind them.

From the other side of the house, Adam heard this hasty exit and winced. That truck was almost new.

Max was playing up well, seeming to take an intense interest in Elliot's confident ramblings on the stock market. Adam noticed for the first time that Max did not look good, his face sallow and unhealthy, stained fingers toying incessantly with a lighted cigarette. Had he always been this thin? Adam couldn't remember. He had never liked Rourke and had therefore ignored him as much as possible. *Not,* he thought wryly, *that I've ever paid much more attention to people I do like.*

Elliot Bentley had at first seemed flattered by their request for advice, submerged in his enthusiasm for his subject. But now, more and more distracted, his gaze kept wandering back to the house, his conversation wandering into vague deadends. Someone came to the back door, said, "Hey, aren't you three going to eat something?"

Bentley seemed to welcome this deliverance. "Well, I'd better see about my wife," he said heartily. "Nice talking to you guys. Hope I've been of some help."

Adam let him go. He'd never catch up to the women now anyway, not the way Genna drove.

Max showed no inclination to go inside. "So what was that all in aid of anyway?" he asked, but didn't seem to expect an answer, because he continued restlessly, "That guy's a fake anyhow; I hope you aren't planning on taking any of that guff for gospel. His own company's just held together by bluff and debt. He's on the skids." He drew heavily on his cigarette, coughed, laughed, "As aren't we all."

"You look it," Adam said.

Max peered at him sharply through the smoke, laughed hoarsely again. "Good old Adam," he said. "Common sense and capitalism. The all-American way. I should put you in one of my books."

"You already did," Adam replied. "Remember? The futuristic one where the human race is furthered by selective artificial insemination."

"Oh, yeah," Max said. "You were one of the managers. A real bore, as I recall."

Leona began to revive when they were halfway to town. She took in Genna, her daughter, and the truck with dumb bewilderment, then uneasiness. "What's wrong?" she shrilled. "Where are we going?"

"Nothing's wrong, Mother," Tanya said. "We're going to see Nancy."

"Nancy! I don't want to see Nancy! Elliot will be . . . upset. Turn around, please, Genna." She put a tentative hand on Genna's arm. "I don't know what idea Tanya has got into her head, but— Nancy and I are much happier not seeing each other."

Genna shook her head without taking her gaze off the road. She felt the other woman's hold tighten convulsively, then, seeming to make a mammoth effort, Leona loosened her grip. The harsh lines in her face smoothed out into a sweet reasonableness.

"I really don't know what Tanya has been telling you, Genna, but you know teenagers. They tend to exaggerate. It was naughty of her to bother you. I don't know why she's got this thing about me reconciling with Nancy, but that should really be my decision, shouldn't it? And today is not a good day for it. I really don't feel very well—"

"This isn't about Nancy, Mother," Tanya said. "You know that. Us teenagers *tend to exaggerate*, do we? You'd make your own daughter out a liar. Well it isn't any use. I've already told Genna everything—and Ellen. I'm going to tell everybody."

"Tanya!" The tone was high and piercing again. "How could you? Don't you care what—"

"What they think?" Tanya interrupted. "No, I don't. I've been trying the truth, and it's made me free just like the Bible says. You do remember *that* part of the Bible, don't you, Mother?"

"How could you do this to me?" Leona breathed. "Tanya, *how could you*? I want to go home now. You can't make me—"

They were entering the outskirts of the town. Genna pulled up to the curb beside a telephone booth, left the motor running, and kept her gaze fixed on the rearview mirror to avoid seeing Leona's pitiful face. *I'm not so much compassionate,* Genna thought, *as squeamish, and that definitely isn't a virtue.*

Leona was crying. She made a sudden lunge across Tanya's lap, reaching for the door handle. Genna punched a button that locked both doors.

"You can't do this!" Leona was screaming. "You can't force me—" A couple women passing on the sidewalk gave the occupants of the truck a startled look and hurried on.

"No, we can't," Tanya agreed calmly. "But listen to me, Mother. *Listen.*" She took her mother's face between her hands. "I am going to get out now and see if I can find Nancy's address. You can get out too, and run away if you want. But, if you do, you will never see me again. Do you understand that? You can go home if you want, but I won't be there. I have a life, Mother, even if you don't. And I'm not going to stick around making myself sick by watching you waste yours. Whatever *you* do, *I'm* going on. And I won't feel guilty. You have your chance now. If you won't take it, there's nothing more I can do for you. All right, Genna."

Genna unlocked the door.

Tanya scrambled down over the running board and, leaving the door open, went, without a backward glance, into the booth.

Genna sat tense, still looking into the mirror. The open door caused the truck to make a warning pinging sound. Leona was moaning quietly to herself. Staring blindly at the stretch of blacktop behind them, Genna waited to feel her move. She could hear the rustling of pages in the telephone book, the loud rap of shoes on the sidewalk as someone walked by between them and the booth. The footsteps hesitated, rapped back. "Are you all right, Mrs. Bentley?" a loud, gruff voice inquired.

Genna jumped, looked around at a stout bankerish looking type in a three-piece suit who was standing by the open door, staring suspiciously at her across Leona.

She saw Tanya, coming out of the booth behind him, pause. "All right?" Leona said finally. "Yes, I'm fine really. All right. Everything's all right." Gripping hands tightly together in her lap, she looked at her daughter.

"Mother will be okay, Mr. Woodley," Tanya said. "Everything's okay." She maneuvered around him up onto the seat, shut the door firmly, took Leona's hands. "Mother," she repeated with only the slightest suspicion of a quaver in her voice, "will be fine."

After milking that evening, Adam felt restless. He had driven Genna's car down from the parsonage, and it still sat in the drive outside the barn. For distraction, he pulled the car into the shop where he repaired his machinery and set to work lifting out the radiator. Still, even wielding the soldering iron, an uneasiness kept creeping into his consciousness, as of something incomplete—something to do with the whole thing about Leona Bentley. Had they handled that right? What would Enoch have done?

He kept glancing at the extension phone on the workbench. Genna would have called if anything had gone wrong, wouldn't she?

It wasn't until he was easing the radiator back into place that it occurred to him. Elliot Bentley. What was he doing? Did he understand what had happened? What was he thinking now?

And I'm worrying about that, Adam thought, disgusted with himself. *That scum doesn't deserve any thought. Any guy who would hit a woman—* With one hand still resting on the front of the car, he reached up with the other to slam the hood.

The thought drove in under his defenses like a fist to the stomach. *Oh, yeah? What about what you did to Genna? You meant to hurt her, and you succeeded, big man. Admit it, with anybody else you would have reacted differently. But she'd dented your ego, and you made her pay, didn't you? Have to admit you're a bit more civilized though. You know how to do it without leaving bruises that can be seen. Proud of yourself, big man?*

Cullen's hand automatically yanked down the hood, and he barely whisked the other out of the way in time to avoid its being smashed.

Leaning on top of that hood, he felt as if he *had* literally been punched: physically nauseated with cold sweat standing out on his forehead. He leaned there for a long time while the fluorescent light over the work-bench flickered and hummed and a dog barked some-where in the distance. Shep sat up to listen to the other animal, decided its message was not important, and looked inquiringly at his master. The collie's tail rustled encouraging on the cement floor.

Finally, Adam straightened up, moved stiffly to the phone, and dialed a number. "Ben?" he said when Gro-ver answered "I think there's something you should

125

know." In a few difficult sentences, he explained about the Bentleys.

The older man was silent after he had finished, said finally, "There's something more, isn't there?"

"Yeah. I was thinking about what Enoch would have done. I think we got to go find Elliot."

He had expected objections, but, after another pause, Grover said with a sigh, "Yeah, I think you're right. Suppose I better drive, huh, since Genna has your truck?"

The phone was shrilling when Adam unlocked his door again around midnight. "Where have you been?" Genna's voice demanded when he picked up the receiver. "I thought our killer must have struck again."

"Really? Were you worried?"

"You bet I was. I have your truck and a blank check in my pocket. Who do you think Lansky would have arrested? I was just contemplating cleaning out your bank account and heading for Mexico. Mexico sounds rather attractive at the moment actually. I could hole up in some little mountain town where nobody speaks English and grow leeks and llamas and be the local mad gringress and nobody would bother me."

She sounded nervy and depressed beneath the bright chatter.

He said, "What's the matter? Wouldn't her sister take her?"

126

"Oh, yes, she fell on her neck like the prodigal's father. Seems Nancy got converted recently and has been trying to think up some way to patch things up with Leona. She was ecstatic; Lansky wasn't, but he seems resigned. I'm sleeping on the couch. Tanya wanted me to hang around for a bit longer in case her father shows up. In which situation I would think that the lieutenant would be more use than me, but you never know."

"Elliot won't be showing up there. He's in the hospital."

"Really?" She sounded too tired to be surprised. "What happened to him?"

"Ben and I found him at a bar out on Route 52. He'd gone all to pieces, was weeping and groveling all over the place. The bartender was glad we showed up, said his customers were getting disgusted."

"Oh," she said. "Were *you*? Disgusted, I mean."

"No. I got smacked with a few home truths about myself tonight, and for the moment, I don't have any extra disgust on hand for anybody else. It's pretty bad when a good hard look at yourself makes you nauseated, isn't it?"

"It is difficult," she agreed drowsily, "finding out that you're not a nice person after all. I remember when it happened to me. It was when your dog was a puppy. He blundered through a bed of very delicate seedlings I'd just set out because he was so eager to see me, and I smacked him for it It suddenly occurred to me that

that's how they show someone is a villain in a book, by having them take out their temper on animals. So then, of course, I had to try to prove to myself that I really wasn't that bad. Only I couldn't. In fact, the harder I tried to dig myself out, the deeper in I got. It was quite devastating. Only then it was something of a relief too.

"Sort of like," she rambled on dreamily, "those wretched heels I was wearing today. They might make my legs look good and give me a little artificial height. But they pinch and warp in the process, not to mention making me all teetery and insecure. Kicking off my delusions about myself was a little *lowering* to begin with, but it got rid of a lot of tension.

"Anyway," she reverted suddenly, "if Shep wants to bury the occasional bone now, I remind myself that perfect gardens are not natural."

"What?" Adam said. "Do you mean that Shep—Why didn't you—"

"Shut up, Cullen," she said distinctly. "I can jolly well let your dog dig up my garden if I want to. It's a free country."

And when he started to laugh, she added with mock dignity, "It is definitely not nice of you to make fun of me when I showed such remarkable Christian fortitude in not even once mentioning this when you were carrying on about Gratis. You will never know the excruciating agonies I suffered I was quite im pressed with myself. It was right up there with burning at the stake, I assure you."

"I'm not making fun of you," he protested. "I think you're wonderful. And incidentally, your legs don't need any help. In looking good, I mean."

She took a moment of silence to contemplate that suspiciously. "Go to bed, Cullen," she said. "You're getting delirious. I'm quite impressed with what you guys did for Elliot too. So impressed that I might actually be back tomorrow instead of heading for Mexico with your life savings. But, just in case, *hasta luego, estupido.* Being interpreted, so long, sucker." And she hung up.

He was still grinning when he rolled into bed. His last thought before sleep was that the burden of what had happened to him that evening had disappeared. In its wake, he felt strangely light, buoyant, as if he had gotten rid of something. "*Adios,* Cullen," he muttered, "and good riddance."

CHAPTER 7

Wherefore is light given to him
that is in misery, and life unto
the bitter in soul . . . Why is
light given to a man whose way
is hid, and whom God hath
hedged in? . . . For the thing
which I greatly feared is come
upon me, and that which I was
afraid of is come unto me. I
was not in safety, neither had I
rest, neither was I quiet; yet
trouble came.
Job 3:20, 23, 25-26

Max Rourke caught a plane to New York City on Thursday evening, checked into a room in a hotel, and went round to all his old haunts on Friday. All his artistic friends seemed aging, sadder, as if they could no longer remember what their purpose in it all was. In their forties, the early diatribes against the materialistic system had thinned under the grinding reality of living on too little money and too much pride. Now those complaints had more than a tinge of sour grapes to their flavor. They resented him, he thought, because he had been a household name for a while, felt secretly gleeful that he was beginning to slide, consoled him a little too enthusiastically on the poor sales of his most recent book.

He went to a boozy party on Friday night, took one of his old girlfriends back to his hotel with him. She was doing well, had abandoned her own writing to become an editor of lurid romances.

"You know what your problem is, Max?" she asked the next morning, sitting at the dresser to apply her makeup. "You never learned to get along with things as they are. So you bury yourself back in the boonies somewhere. And, from your books, I'd say the people there aren't any more to your liking than here. Why do you think that is?"

"Because they get along with things as they are?" he quoted wearily.

"That's right! But you just never learn. I mean, your kind of attitude is standard for kids, but there comes a time to grow up, you know."

"Really?" He squinted against the smoke of his cigarette.

"Really. You're a closet idealist, Max. Face up to it. You have the expectations of an eighteen year old, and you sulk like one when things go wrong. I saw that latest effort of yours when it came to our company, you know. You really deep-down have a grudging admiration for that preacher; that's why none of the venom rang true. You're still looking for somebody to save the world."

"Had," he said.

"What?"

"*Had* a grudging admiration for that preacher. He got murdered."

She turned, frowning. "Who killed him?"

"Who knows? Everybody hopes it was his neurotic cousin. Or me. They're really not too picky which."

"And you left the state when you're under suspicion? Do you want them to haul you back in chains?"

"It might be amusing," he said. "So few things are amusing anymore."

"Including me, I suppose," she said.

"No offense meant," he said, "but you've become a colossal bore."

"I could say the same of you." She picked up her handbag and glanced at the clock. "Well, it's been nice, or not, as the case may be."

He continued to sit, cross-legged, on the bed until he'd finished his cigarette. Maybe he had secretly, wistfully admired the old man's sense of purpose. He was willing to admit that now because the old man had been wrong, hadn't he? He who had been so sure of a reason behind things had gone to a senseless death, probably at the hands of his mentally unbalanced cousin. Just as the one he'd called Master had supposedly died at the hands of some jealous—and religious—politicians. Senseless.

His drinking the night before had left Max with a light but constant headache, a sour taste in his mouth.

But he could almost wish for a more intense pain—just to be able to feel. The old hotel had windows that opened, and Max forced his up to clear out the stuffiness, the staleness in the room and in his brain.

He leaned on the sill, looking with something like curiousity down seven stories to the alley below. One would certainly feel something after that drop—for a brief instant before oblivion. He wasn't taking the idea seriously, or thought he wasn't. He had only opened the window for air. But some fascination kept him there, bent over the sill, choking back his breathing, making him dizzy. Make one last statement, one final rebellion to it all? The only life worth living, the preacher had said once, is an extreme one, a passion for one side or the other. Sin had become a bore, but he didn't have the nerve for the other. After years of exposing the guilt and folly of his fellow human beings, he no longer had the strength to believe in anything else—to turn around, even to turn back into the room again. So he leaned precariously, feeling trapped, smothered, pushed.

The sudden knocking on his door startled him so that he jerked and almost overbalanced. Panicked, he threw himself hard backward and banged his head on the overhead sash. He found himself crouched, panting, on the floor of what seemed like a different room. His every movement brought flashes of pain, and the objects in the room that had seemed so cheap and banal stood out with an excruciating vividness. The bedspread jangled with color; the cheap seascape on the wall vibrated with light. A rush of air from the window burned into his throat and lungs with cold fire. Somebody was standing behind him looking down at him; he was sure of it even though he was right up against the wall and there was no room. He crawled painfully away, as if the providing of space would make it more rational. He refused to look back. The knocking came again. Holding onto his head with one hand, he staggered up and across to the door, threw it open, and screamed, "What?"

A myopic little priest peered at him with a mildly startled air, looked back down at a paper, then at the door. "Oh, I am sorry," the cleric said. "I read that wrong. I'm looking for 883, see, not 888." He extended the paper helpfully.

Rourke ignored it, continuing to glare and sway. "Are you all right, sir?" the priest inquired. "You look—" Max slammed the door so hard that it bounced a little way open again, and he went to sit on the bed while pain exploded like rockets inside his skull. "Funny!" he growled at someone, "A priest yet. Verr-ry funny!"

When the pain had at last subsided somewhat, it left him fully alert, thinking hard—and wary. The room had settled a little, but still seemed alive. This must be a nervous breakdown. He was exhibiting all the symptoms of schizophrenia. Actually it seemed more like a breakthrough than a breakdown. So might an infant wince now, as he was wincing, against the clarity of light

135

and sound in its new peculiar world. He tried to remember what he'd been thinking about. Senselessness. It seemed suddenly safe, sane, and he made a last despairing grab at it. He would get that mousy little woman to talk; she was the type to crack under pressure. Head down, he groped cautiously for the telephone, began dialing information.

Ellen came into the parsonage in mid-morning, lugging a large, awkward package. She had been down to Genna's to pick up Enoch's portrait. The artist had called to ask, irritably, if Ellen would like to have it. "It's taking up space," Genna had said, "and I certainly can't sell it."

The sun was shining, and outside the daffodils nodded in a fresh breeze. Inside, someone had left a small plate of cookies on the table. People had been leaving plates of food ever since Enoch died, but most of that had stopped after the funeral feast.

Ellen carried the painting into the little room that had been Enoch's study, leaned it against the desk, and went back out to the kitchen to get a hammer and nail from one of the drawers. Feeling the pangs of mid-morning hunger, she carried the plate of cookies back with her. They were big, soft, and golden-brown with M & M chocolate-covered peanuts in them. She chewed while she considered where to hang the painting. Right above the desk, she decided and laid the cookie down, half-eaten, while she climbed on a straight-backed chair to drive a nail into the wall.

A breeze ruffled her skirts and papers on the desk, a board creaked in the hall. She stopped for a moment, listening. "Anybody there?" she called.

When silence was the only answer, she decided that the wind must have blown one of the doors open. They never latched very well.

She bent to lift the painting. The breeze had stopped. Maybe it wasn't the door after all. Old houses tended to be as drafty as they were rustic. She slipped the picture wire over the nail, slid the wire along until the top of the painting looked even with the line of the ceiling, stepped down and back to take a look. The problem was that the ceiling line was not even with the floor line. She climbed back up to adjust the picture's frame to an acceptable compromise between the two. Down on the floor again, she picked up her cookie, nodded her head positively. Enoch had returned to his place.

He looked down at her with that twinkle that suggested the sharing of some stupendous joke, and she had to smile in return. She finished her cookie, reached absently for another. Aunt Katherine would say that she was spoiling her lunch. But there was no rule to say that one had to eat lunch! She and Enoch smiled together again at that. Not if one had a whole plate of delicious cookies. Except—that they weren't so delicious. She stopped and frowned at the remains of the one in her hand. Thus far she had been eating inattentively, but now. . . There was a bitter taste at the back of her throat. Bitter. There hadn't been any note with those cookies, nothing to say who had brought them. So someone had goofed up a recipe. *Don't start again, Ellen.*

Then, behind her, the door to the study slammed. She whirled, fear rising in her throat. *The wind*, her mind caught at that excuse again, but then she heard the sound of the key turning in the lock. The wind couldn't turn keys.

She dropped the rest of the second cookie, backed away from it and the door until she was behind the desk. She had asked Enoch once why the door to the study locked from the outside and he hadn't known. It had been a nursery, perhaps, he suggested. It had been added after the house was built, carved out of one of the bigger rooms, so that there were no windows and only the one door. He had liked it because it freed him from distractions. He was easily distracted, and often joked that she should lock him in until he was done preparing his sermon.

No other doors. No windows. No other way out. And poison burning in her throat.

The paralyzing fear she had thought herself rid of surged back in force. *Nothing you can do*, it said. *Nothing.* She moved as quietly as possible, loath that that thing out there should hear her. She fancied she could see the shadow of its feet under the door.

She crouched behind the desk, glanced up at the portrait. *Enoch, help me!*

There was something else about the study, something else about distractions. The telephone! Or the lack of one since, after she had come, Enoch had disconnected the extension in the study—when there was someone else to answer the shrill summons.

Where she crouched, she could see the empty plug that had given it life, that might give her life if it were here now. What had he done with it?

An organized person would have taken it away, out of this tiny room, where all available space was needed. But Enoch hadn't been an organized sort. She began to pull frantically at the desk doors, to paw through notebooks and scribbled papers.

Any minute now, she might feel the poison starting to take effect, feel its weakness in her limbs, its strangling fingers at her throat. She yanked out the big bottom drawer with an effort. It was warped, full of odds and ends: an old pencil sharpener, pencil stubs, pens that didn't write anymore. Discards. Perhaps then. . . And there it was under a last dusty pile of papers—thrust to the bottom, as if to still its noisy clangor forever.

But, even as she lifted it out, fumbled shakily with the plug, she didn't feel hope, but merely that she was staving off the inevitable for just a few more minutes. She wondered if that thing out there could see her. Was its eye bent to the keyhole to watch the last writhings of its catch?

The plug went in and the phone rang. Ellen stared at it dully, then lifted the receiver. "I've been poisoned," she said.

At the other end, Max Rourke gaped. Had the woman gone completely round the bend already?

"Did you hear me?" Her voice rose hysterically. "I've been poisoned! I found some cookies on the kitchen table and I ate a couple, and they were bitter. And then someone locked me in the study here. What shall I do?"

"How long ago did you eat them?" he asked stupidly, staring at his own face in the mirror across the room.

"I don't know. A few minutes ago, I guess."

"All right," he said, suddenly brisk. "Listen. Put your finger down your throat and throw them up."

Silence. "Did you hear me?"

A wail. "I can't do it! I can't!"

"Would you rather be dead?" he asked brutally. "With six feet of dirt on your face? You don't, and you'll never eat anything again, get me? Do it!"

Silence again, then a retching sound. And through it, he heard a slight click, as of someone picking up another phone. "Ellen. Ellen, can you hear me!"

Her voice sounded weaker. "I did it."

"Did you get it all up?"

"I think so."

"Do you have a party line there?"

"No, Enoch always wanted people to be able to get through to him." She didn't ask why.

He hoped she couldn't feel, as he did, the breathing of evil there on the other end of hundreds of miles of line, in that house with her. Then another click.

He felt hugely helpless. "Listen! Can you find something heavy?"

There was a tap on his half-open door. The little priest poked his head around it. "Excuse me, sir, but are you sure you're really all r—"

Rourke beckoned frantically to him, scooped up a memo pad from the phone table, began scribbling on it. The priest advanced cautiously.

"There's a big paperweight on the desk," Ellen said.

"All right," he said. "That's fine; that's great! Pick it up. Get it in your hand!"

In an aside to the priest, he said, "Get to another phone and call up the ambulance in this town. Tell them to get out to the parsonage in Deerfield. They'll know where it's at; they were at the church a couple days ago. Tell them a woman's been poisoned and is locked in one of the inner rooms.

"No," he said into the phone to Ellen. "I don't think whoever it is will come in. Poisoners don't have that much nerve. But be ready anyhow."

And to the priest. "After you've done that, call the state cops in the same town. Get a Lieutenant Lansky if you can. Tell him Ellen Foster's been poisoned. Got that? Then get going!"

After a final keenly assessing glance, the little man nodded briskly and scurried out.

"Ellen, you still there? You still have that paperweight?"

"Yes."

"Okay, fine. If somebody does come in, stay there behind the desk. Make them come to you. And don't use that until they're up close. Unless they have a gun. Then you'll have to throw it at the gun."

"I couldn't hit a gun from here," Ellen protested.

"Well, throw it at the arm then," he snapped. "Or the shoulder. Or the groin, if it's a man. Just hit them somewhere! Where did you say you got those cookies?"

"On the kitchen table," she said. "Somebody left them there when I was out."

He drew breath. "And you *ate* them? Less than a week after your cousin was poisoned, some anonymous donor leaves you cookies, and you *eat* them? Do you ever use your brain for anything other than a hat rack?"

Ellen Foster was suddenly, brilliantly, angry. Furious, in fact. "I do not have to listen to this," she said, and hung up. She stood, dusted her skirt briskly with one hand, sat down in the desk chair, and looked at the door, hefting the paperweight in one small hand and waiting.

Rourke swore, punched out the number for information again with clumsy fingers. The priest had come back, was lingering by the door. "Well?" Max snapped at him.

"Mission accomplished," the little man reported with some smugness.

"What did Lansky do?" Max asked, and, to the operator, "get me a number for Adam Cullen."

"A great deal of swearing actually," the priest said. "Though I could hear him yelling out a few orders in between. Then he asked who I was. When I told him that I was Father Brown from New York City, he didn't seem convinced, so I added that I had been given the information by Mr. Max Rourke. He seemed a bit incensed about your being here." Brown reflected. "He seemed incensed about everything actually."

The writer was too busy stabbing out a number again to pay much attention, listening to a far off empty-sounding ring with a feeling of futility. No self-respecting farmer would be indoors in mid-morning anyway.

Then "Hello," with the loud noise of some machinery in the background. Bless the man; he had extension phones! "This is Max Rourke. Ellen Foster's been poisoned. She's locked in the study, and the murderer's in the house with her somewhere. Get over there."

"Okay," and a click. Bless the man for being short on words too.

"Well, we've done all we can," Rourke said, hanging up and running a shaking hand through his already wild hair. "Did you say Father Brown?"

"As in Chesterton," the little cleric agreed. "I get a lot of teasing about it."

"I'll bet. How did you know my name?"

"I saw you on a talk show once. I said a prayer for you at the time, I think. You seemed, if you don't mind my saying, a most confused young man."

Rourke looked from the window to the priest to the telephone with the sly, desperate caution of a fox hearing the hounds closing in. The kaleidescope colors of the insane were falling clickingly into an intricate pattern. "It's all some kind of plot, isn't it?" he said thickly.

Unperturbed, the little priest smiled, "What Chesterton called the most daring of conspiracies," he replied cheerfully.

Max paced and rang the hospital every few minutes until a nurse finally told him that Ellen Foster had been admitted, had had her stomach pumped, and would live, and to stop bothering them. The little priest sat on the bed and watched him placidly.

"I don't know why I bothered," Max said savagely. "I don't like this. I—" He looked at his hands and shook his head.

"You don't like worrying about someone?" the priest supplied. "Why?"

Max shook his head again, at a loss for words. "It's

. . . sticky," he muttered finally. "I don't like stickiness." Impatiently, "Never mind. You wouldn't understand!"

"Oh, it's a common enough attitude," the priest said. "And quite atheistic, though some would be shocked to know that. I imagine you would have felt better about it if you'd had some attraction to the woman, wouldn't you?"

Max looked at him. "Don't you have somewhere more important to be?" he asked.

The priest considered that. "No," he said simply. And went on, "Because then you could explain it away. It's strange, isn't it, that explaining is usually an attempt to get something out of one's way."

"I'm not sticking around here!" Max said with disgust, looking around for his suitcase. "What's the point? My friends are as much materialists now as the Wall Street junkies. I don't belong here anymore. They used to—"

"Believe in something?" Brown suggested. "But just what was it that they believed in?" When Rourke didn't answer, he continued, "Art perhaps? Art has become a rather vague term, you know. Themselves? Anyone with a sense of humor gets over that one pretty fast. To quote Chesterton again, 'Only a rotter believes in himself.' So what else did you expect from them?"

"A little courage," the writer replied.

"Courage enough to face a godless universe?" the priest asked. "But that doesn't take courage, Max. That only takes resignation. And you aren't resigned, are you?

"That's what I like about atheism," Brown went on. "That it isn't indifferent. We may be on opposite sides, but at least we care—one way or another. Our difference is that you're still hoping that man can make it on his own, and we know that he can't."

Max pulled his suitcase out from under the bed, began hurling clothes into it. "You prove this God of yours to me, padre," he said. "And maybe I'll listen."

"There's only ever been one sure method of proving anything," the other man retorted. "And that's trying it for yourself."

Max laughed scornfully. "Yeah, Father," he said, "just like taking a flying leap off a cliff when you can't see the bottom. Fat chance!"

The priest got up and wandered to the door. "Can it be that the man's afraid?" he asked the doorknob softly. Then, as he turned his head, Max saw Enoch Foster's irrepressible laughter in Father Brown's eyes. "I double dast dare you, Max Rourke," the priest said solemnly.

It was perhaps fortunate that two policemen in a prowl car reached the parsonage first. And that, as was their custom, they announced their identity before unlocking and throwing open the study door—guns at the ready. Otherwise one of them might have been the recipient of an angry paperweight in a sensitive spot. As it was, Ellen quietly put her weapon down on the desk.

Two ambulance attendants came in then with Adam Cullen and Genna, whom Adam had picked up along the way. Two hours later, Ellen was propped up by pillows in a hospital bed, looking pale but still angry. Genna had ridden down in the ambulance with her; Adam had followed in his truck. They were waiting for Lieutenant Lansky, who had had the cookies rushed to the police lab for analysis.

"Well, you don't want to be too upset with the man," Genna was saying of Max Rourke. "I mean, he does seem to have saved your life."

"That," Ellen Foster said, "is no excuse for his kind of rudeness. Why do people put up with him anyway?"

A big police officer leaned against the wall outside the open door. Looking at him, Ellen choked furiously, "And why does someone try to kill me? What did I ever do? And what are the police doing—trying to discover this murderer by waiting until everybody else is eliminated?"

Genna patted her soothingly and eased the table away from the bedside. In her present mood, Ellen might start chucking a water pitcher or Kleenex box at the officer. Standing at the window, Adam Cullen said, "Well, we can eliminate Max at any rate."

"So it wasn't in the juice after all," Rhys said wonderingly. "But how—"

"It could have been anytime that morning then,"

Lansky fumed. "And there goes our list of suspects. Now, it could be anybody in the county! I mean, just consider how many were at that sunrise service alone!"

"There would have to be some other way of administering it though," Rhys said. "I mean, nobody said anything about cookies that morning."

"It wouldn't have to be a cookie," the lieutenant came back, "A sweet roll would have done. He had a sweet tooth, remember. Wait a minute. Something—"

He held up a hand, frowning in intense concentration. "Sweets, something about—" The frown ironed out. "No, I was just remembering a basket some kid left. That wouldn't have anything—"

"Left where?" Rhys asked.

"In the church that morning!" Lansky snapped. "It's not important!"

"There weren't any kids in the church that morning," Rhys said. "Remember? I mean, there might have been some there beforehand, but they had their own service—"

Lansky was staring. "Kids," he muttered. "Sweet tooth. Angels. Come on! Let's get over to the hospital!"

"The lab boys almost missed it," he told the three in the room, "because it wasn't in the batter after all, but ir the nuts."

"In the nuts?" Adam asked. "You mean injected, or something?"

"No," the policeman replied. "I mean beans. Literally. Precatory beans. The boys had never heard of them, had to look them up. But I imagine you had, Miss Leon. Heard of them, I mean."

"Yes," she said, "I didn't include them in my talk because they don't grow around here. Only down south somewhere, I think. And one of them is enough to kill an adult. Am I right?"

Without waiting for an answer, she mused, "They're red with a tinge of black, and they're used to make necklaces. But how did Enoch—"

Ellen interrupted; she had gone, if possible, whiter. "I think I know who the murderer is then, Lieutenant."

"So do I," he said. "If I'm right about a couple things. What do you know about construction paper baskets with chocolate candy?"

The two women exchanged glances. "Our ladies' auxiliary made those," Genna said. "To be passed out to the children at their service on Sunday. We even dipped the candy ourselves. Why?"

Lansky ignored the question. "Miss Foster, did your cousin ever make paper dolls?"

The woman looked at him dubiously. "Dolls?"

"Cut out," he gestured with his hands. "In a chain."

Her face cleared. "Oh, yes, he did that sometimes

when he was thinking, claimed it helped him concentrate. Only he usually made angels."

The lieutenant was grinning broadly. "So the children didn't get the candy until they were in their service, and none of them had left that service before the murder occurred. But what if someone had gone into the church where Foster was studying his sermon beforehand, someone who had a good excuse to be there, and offered him one of those baskets? What would his reaction have been?"

The two women exchanged glances again. Both of them looked sick. "He would have been delighted, I imagine," Ellen said stiffly.

"And?"

"And—" She struggled hoarsely to go on, finished in a whisper, putting a hand over her face, "He would have eaten one or two to show his gratitude."

Lansky turned to Genna. "There were some nuts, I suppose, in some of that candy?"

The artist was looking down at the hands clenched together in her lap. "Peanut clusters," she said.

"And if some of those peanuts had tasted a little bitter?" the policeman continued with that same relentless cheerfulness.

"He wasn't the type to complain," Adam Cullen said.

Genna stirred. "So it wasn't the chalice after all?"

"No, we should have known. Only cyanide could have worked that fast, and it wasn't cyanide. He probably felt some symptoms there towards the end. Crawling on the skin, nausea, shakiness. But, like we know already, he'd had the flu, that service was important to him, and he wasn't the type to complain."

"So, Miss Leon, did you talk to anybody about precatory beans?"

She was still looking down; her nod was barely perceptible.

Standing with his hands on the back of her chair, Adam repeated, "Somebody who had a good reason to be there," and nodded in sudden comprehension. "But what's the motive?"

"Who?" exploded Rhys. "*Who*? Will somebody let me in on that?"

CHAPTER 8

Ye are of your father the devil,
and the lusts of your father ye
will do. He was a murderer
from the beginning, and abode
not in the truth, because there
is no truth in him.
John 8:44

Genna argued with Adam on the way home. The latter part was more a harangue than an argument, though, since the farmer had by then lapsed into tight-lipped silence. He let her out at the end of her drive, and by the time Genna reached the house, she could not remember what had started the disagreement. It was typical, she thought, that when she wanted a real noisy quarrel, the wretched man wouldn't give her one!

She was tired and dispirited and suspected that she was coming down with something. The police had gone out to make an arrest even before she and Adam left the hospital, but she tried not to think of that.

The fire in her wood stove had gone out, and she shoved some paper in amongst the gray coals, lay some wood over it. Then she couldn't find matches.

Finally she gave up the fire, wandered listlessly across to the couch, and dumped piles of books on the floor. The books, she noticed, as a card fell out of one, were overdue.

She lay down, curling up tight under a flimsy afghan for warmth. They had picked up supper at a fast-food drive-in on the way home, and the greasy fare lay heavy in her stomach. Adam would be up there starting his milking. Would he be angry with her or just generally disgusted? *You really should grow up, Genna*, she thought.

Grimm had been expressing displeasure over her long absence by stalking up and down the room, mrr-owing, thrashing his tail, and knocking things about. When he found that she was paying no attention to him, he went to lie on her stomach and glare into her dis-tracted face.

The gray light in the room deepened subtly as Genna's thoughts drifted gradually into incoherence and dream pictures. She was wakened by a drowsily curious, "Mrrrr?" from the cat. She felt its weight shift, melt away, and heard the padded thud of its paws hitting the floor. She felt the sickish, pasty-mouthed lethargy that was her body's way of punishing her for sleeping at the wrong time. It had gotten awfully hot; the fire must have started up again after all; she could hear its snapping. She shoved the afghan away, started to sit up. The cat yelped, with outrage, as he did when she stepped on his foot or tail. A flash of movement passed her in the dark as he leaped back onto the couch, grumbling.

Swinging her feet to the floor, Genna shook her head to clear it, frowned, shook her head again. He was probably just hungry. She stood, cautiously, because sudden waking tended to make her dizzy. Another noise across the room: a muffled clatter of books tumbling. She almost said, "Grimm!" before she remembered that he was behind her. She reached to make sure, patting empty space before her hand finally fumbled onto his fur. He emitted a hoarse, automatic purr, but his body felt tense, preoccupied.

Those rats again! she thought with disgust. She'd hoped the poison had gotten them all. The package had said it would drive them out of the house in search of water before they died, but she had stepped on one in the basement the day before, one that had writhed and squealed under her foot. She didn't want to experience that again. Especially in the dark.

She edged sideways, reaching tentatively with her foot to locate obstacles before each step. She hoped it wouldn't rush suddenly her way. But who knew what a poison-crazed rodent would do? She felt the hair crawl at the back of her neck.

Just rodents after all, she told herself. *Just furry little creatures. Like squirrels, only squirrels happen to be cuter. Just because they have bigger eyes and bushy tails. Rats aren't malicious after all. Just scavengers—like squirrels.*

And they would scurry at the first sign of light. Something brushed her leg, and she almost shrieked. But then she heard the faint, tense purr again. Grimm. Her reaching hand brushed the table where her paint tubes lay; something oily smeared across her finger. She had forgotten to cap one of them again. The scuffling noise was moving almost parallel with her, but away, toward the couch. She had lost her bearings in the dark, was still far from the light switch, but there was a small lamp attached to the top of her easel. Again she groped with empty space, leaned further and further until she almost overbalanced. Her hand knocked finally painfully against the canvas. It tipped against her chest.

Over by the couch, that indeterminate noise stopped, as if something were listening. Then it resumed, even more quietly, only a slight whisper of movement.

She followed the wood of the easel up to the lamp, stroked the smooth metal surface, searching for the chain. Strange that she had used it so often, but she couldn't remember where the chain was. Strange what the dark could do to your mind.

She forced herself to go more slowly, more carefully over every inch of the metal till her fingers found the bump where the chain went in, slid down to close gratefully around the chain itself. She looked over her shoulder in the direction of the couch, yanked.

There was no scuttling retreat. Instead a shadowy figure bending over the couch jerked up and half-turned to look at her. The light was not strong, and that figure stood at the edge of its radiance, but Genna recognized who it was easily enough. So close to the lamp itself that she could feel its warmth on her hair, she said, "Hello, Meredith. What are you doing here?"

The other woman did not look as much startled as angry. "I should have known," she said. "You never fail to mess things up, Genna. And I was so careful too. I waited and waited until you were sure to be sound asleep."

Grimm was sitting on Genna's foot. "The cat woke me," she said. She was amazingly calm despite the gun that Meredith was holding in one hand, close in against a beautifully tailored skirt.

Meredith looked at the cat with the same disgust. She had never liked pets.

The whole setting, the whole situation, was just too stagy. "What were you planning on doing with that?" Genna asked, aware that their lines were too trivial for such a confrontation.

"What do you think?" the other asked impatiently.

"But why?" the artist asked with genuine puzzle-ment, rubbing her thumb over the paint on her finger. "What would it get you?"

"Suicide," Meredith explained in an exaggeratedly

157

patient tone. "Everybody knows you're rather strange. Suicide out of remorse or fear. That cop doesn't like you; he would jump at it."

"He knows it was you," Genna said, but almost absently, looking at the smears on her hand.

The other woman shook her head reprovingly. "Not even a good try," she said. "I didn't have any reason—or none that he knows about. It was Garth—"

"What did Garth do?"

Meredith's hand tightened on the gun. "What did he do? *What did he do?*" Her other hand appealed to Genna. "I had it so well planned. You know that. How much we would make each year, how much we should invest. It was perfect, perfect but for one thing. I made the mistake of letting Garth handle the actual money. I mean, I told him what to do with it. All he had to do was carry through. Men have this macho thing, you know, about wanting to be in charge, and I figured that was harmless; I could let him have that."

"He didn't invest in the right things?" Genna hazarded.

"Oh, he did what I told him, all right," Meredith said. "He just decided to try a bit of his own on the side."

"Oh."

"He lost, of course, and then he panicked. He always panics. He didn't want me to find out so he tried to recoup the losses. Kept trying till everything was gone."

"But what did that have to do with Enoch?" Genna asked. And then "Meredith, Garth *didn't*—"

"Yes, he did," the other said. "The church money. He fully planned on paying it back, of course, just as soon—" She trailed off, shrugged her shoulders. "He came crawling to me Saturday morning, like he always does when he gets in trouble. Everything was gone, and Enoch had found out."

The artist looked like a child in the lamplight, tousled hair, wide eyes. "And for that you killed two people? Don't tell me Garth did it, because I know better."

Meredith laughed. "Anybody who knows him would know better," she said contemptuously. "Why I ever married that— I had to kill Enoch, Genna. Surely you realize that I didn't have any choice. I tried to talk to him first, tried to get him to keep it secret, promised we would pay it all back eventually. But he wouldn't listen. He said maybe if it had been his money, but it wasn't. It belonged to the church, and the trustees, at least, would have to know." She laughed again. "As if I would stand for that. There's a lot you can do on bluff and credit, but when people know—

"I had to act fast, of course. He was going to call that meeting of the trustees for Sunday afternoon. It worked out even better than I'd thought, him keeling over like that just after he drank from the chalice. Stealing it was an inspired move on my part, but that greasy little farmhand saw me. You—" she said accusingly, "you did something with that cup, didn't you? Ellen wouldn't have had the nerve. And then when I got it all set up on Adam, you interfered again.

"So it really is your fault, Genna, what's going to happen. If you'd just let it go—"

She was bringing the gun up, and the other woman, straightening the smeared canvas on the easel, said, "You really don't expect them to believe I shot myself from a dozen feet away, do you?"

"Of course not," Meredith said. "I'll come across to you. Stay there."

She doesn't seem mad, Genna thought, *but then maybe it's like somebody said, that madness is a small rational circle. With everything else excluded.* Meredith half-tripped over a roll of canvas, looked down. Genna reached up, yanked the lamp chain, and stepped blindly away into the renewed dark

"Genna!" the other said sharply. "Genna, don't be stupid!"

Stupid, Genna thought to herself, stepping quietly as she had stepped before, holding her skirts up to keep them from rustling against anything. *As if standing placidly still waiting to get shot is the epitome of intelligence.* She reached a wall and edged along it. Ahead she thought she could discern a lighter, grayer spot in the wall. A vertical rectangle that was surely a window although it wavered and darkened even as she stared. Impatient to get closer, she moved incautiously, knocked against a table leg. An explosion ripped apart the rustling silence. Grimm raced past her at speed, leapt for the table; something fell heavily, and a second explosion followed close on the first. She winced, stood still a moment, then, biting her lip, began to ease around the table.

She tried to figure which window it would be. Some of them were so warped that they wouldn't open at all—or only with an awful screech. And some were so loose in the frame that they had to be propped open.

There was no time to figure it out. Meredith might find that lamp on the easel any minute now, or another light switch. Standing to one side of the window, Genna ran her fingertips down the cold glass to the sill, back up to the sash. Drawing a harsh breath, she tugged urgently.

The window shot up with an ease that nearly threw her off balance, banged at the top. She rolled over the sill. The crack of the window falling shut, of a third shot, and her impact with the earth seemed to come as one stunning blow, and she lay, gulping cold air into searing lungs.

Then she scrabbled up onto her feet and began to run. The shell of unreality had been cracked by her fall, and she was suddenly afraid. She went up the lane like a rabbit, shoulders hunched as against a blow, quivering.

She had taken her shoes off when she lay down on the couch, and now ran in stocking feet over uneven gravel and tufts of grass. Slipping, stubbing her toes, down abruptly on skinned hands and knees as her feet spun out from under her, pain sprouting everywhere, a bullet bouncing off a stone in front of her and only hearing the shot as she lurched up again. The lane was impossibly long, and she cut off of it and across a field toward the back of Adam's trailer. It was dark—no lights showing. Had he gone somewhere then? Was she alone here, running and running because you always kept running as long as you could. But running toward nothing?

Something small and dark brushed frantically across her ankles. She tripped over it in a kind of inevitable slow motion, went down into a small gully, engulfed in the cold, vital smell of grass and mud. The chill water stung her hands like fire. A frightened "Mrrr—" An urgent pressing against her skirts. Poor Grimm. Frightened and confused, turning to the only help he knew.

A fresh wind in her face. She pushed back on her knees, rubbed her hands clean on her clothes. Panic had drained away. She continued to give her hands attention, rubbing fastidiously. Then, slowly, calmly, she stood, picked up Grimm, and began to walk on toward the trailer. Without looking back, she could feel Meredith slowing up too, as if suspicious of this sudden change.

The wind came hard down across the open field, hard, cold, and clean. Above its rush, Genna scarcely heard the next shot or the pinging ricochet from the side of the trailer. But she turned automatically, almost absently away to her right, heading for the barn.

Having just finished with his milking, Adam stood, looking around, reassuring himself that everything was complete. He had been preoccupied all evening. She had been trying to make him mad; he'd known that at the time. And yet, despite that knowing, she had succeeded. He heard—and didn't hear—the sound of a shot. In the country, shots were common. Shep, lying in the center aisle, lifted his head and pricked up his ears. After a moment, he got up and went to stand by the door, looking back at his master.

Adam was still preoccupied. Another shot. The dog growled softly. The man looked around, surprised. Shep looked at him insistently.

"All right," Adam said, walking toward the door, reaching for the light switch. His hand paused. Shooting—after dark? He slammed down the switch and threw open the door.

The security light at the front of the trailer illuminated the gravel drive. A woman limped around a corner of the trailer, out of the shadows into the light, carrying a dark cat that clung urgently to her shoulder. She saw him and began to pick her way toward him across the gravel.

He ran to meet her. Another woman came around the opposite, the far end, of the trailer into the light. This one was carrying a gun.

Adam tried to shove Genna behind him. "Don't be silly," she said in a normal tone, but she kept one hand on his arm for support. "You can't shoot both of us, Meredith," she said when the other came to a stop under the light. "You've used five shells already. You've only got one left."

The other woman just stood there, very still, looking at them.

Shep, growling, advanced with a mincing step, hackles raised. She ignored him.

"They knew it was you," Genna continued, chattily, "because of the tulips. They know now that it was in the candy somebody gave him before the service. And you must have been there before because of the tulips. You didn't come in till halfway through the service, but the tulips were already there."

Adam was estimating the distance between himself and Meredith. Not far enough that she was likely to miss, but far enough that she could easily pull the trigger before he reached her.

"And of course there was that red and black necklace of yours," Genna rambled on. "I suppose that's why you tried to kill Ellen. That remark she made about it's not being appropriate. But she really didn't know. She was just making conversation. You panicked, Meredith. I suppose you meant that to look like suicide too, but it wouldn't have worked. Just like this won't. Because they know. You can't hide in the crowd anymore. You never could really."

Meredith began to move, sideways, keeping parallel

to them. Adam watched her hand. The cat still clung to Genna, looking back over its shoulder, eyes gleaming. The dog edged sideways too, keeping carefully between Meredith and the others. It was no longer growling though; its tension had eased.

The woman's grip on the gun seemed to have loosened too, as if she were already forgetting it to other considerations. "I'm going to take the truck," she said. "Give me the keys, Adam. Toss them."

As he watched her drive away down the lane, Adam thought dryly that she was, at any rate, a better driver than Genna. He turned to look at the latter, found her sitting down on the gravel. "You can't sit there," he said then, "What's that?" as he crouched to peer urgently at the rust-colored stain on the front of her blouse.

She giggled. "Not blood. It's paint. A painting that wasn't going very well. Fortunately." She reached up to rub at her eyes, left another trail of red across her cheek.

"Come on," he said. "Get up. That loony dame might decide to come back."

"Doesn't matter." She giggled again. "Only one bullet. That was clever of me, wasn't it?"

"Not particularly," he said. "That was an automatic, not a revolver. Automatics have seven bullets."

"Really?" She didn't seem much interested. When he tried to take her hand to pull her up, she shied away violently.

"Leave me alone. My feet hurt."

He bent again to look at her feet. There was red on her socks that wasn't paint. He lifted her, found that she was trembling violently. The cat transferred its claws from her shoulder to his. He winced, muttered something to himself.

In the trailer, he put her down on the couch, locked the door, drew the curtains, and called the police. Curled up on her side, Genna said, without opening her eyes, through chattering teeth, "Tell them that Garth took all the church money. They'd better get him too."

Adam watched her as he talked to a brisk, professional voice on the other end of the line, and his tone was not friendly. The dispatcher was conciliatory. "Mrs. DeWitt wasn't there when they went to pick her up," he explained. "They've been looking all evening."

"Well, then, just maybe," Adam murmured, "they could have warned us, hmmmm?"

The dispatcher agreed hastily that someone had definitely erred there. "Uh, I suppose you know the license number of your truck, sir?" he suggested tentatively.

When he was done, Adam replaced the receiver with definite emphasis, went to the sink, made a great clatter of moving dirty dishes and running water into a dishpan.

"Temper," Genna murmured chidingly, opening her eyes to look at his back.

He didn't respond, but went away towards the back of the trailer, and she heard him rummaging loudly in the bathroom there. His snapped, "Up!" when he returned, roused her out of a half-doze. Most of her shaking had subsided.

She sat up, groggily, to find him crouched beside his dishpan on the floor. She barely had time to squint at the steaming water through curious, heavy-lidded eyes, before he stripped off her socks and plunged both feet into it. She yelped and attempted to jerk the offended members back without success. His big hands were surprisingly gentle though, and although she said, "Sadistic brute," she said it with a drowsy lack of conviction.

"I feel sorry for Meredith in a way," she confided to his bent head. "I mean, she always knew what she wanted. And then to have it all taken away like that. It doesn't seem fair."

"You should be sorry for Garth," he growled. "Having to live with that woman."

She shook her head. "I was so scared, and then I wasn't. Because I was hanging onto God with all my claws just like Grimm was hanging onto me. And Meredith, she's always been too scared to hang onto anyone but herself. She looks so sufficient, but she's always been so scared of what they would say, of what they would know about her. I think it was that she was afraid of more than anything. What people would say." She shivered. "People aren't very nice. Really."

"Killing people isn't very nice either," Adam said, lifting her feet out of the pan and toweling them dry.

She bit her lip as he applied a stinging antiseptic to

her cuts. "I know. I'm getting all maudlin and weepy, aren't I? It must be a reaction to everything." He replaced her socks with a dry pair of his own. Plucked a blanket from the back of the couch to wrap around her.

"Sit tight," he said. "I'll try to find you a clean shirt. You should get out of those muddy things."

Peering up at him out of her cocoon, she managed a rueful smile. "I'm sorry, Adam. I'm getting to be an awful nuisance, aren't I?" He went away without answering. She bit her lip and tried to smile at the dog that watched her solemnly from the floor. When the man returned, she said, "Never mind. Just find me some boots or something, and I'll toddle off home."

"No way," he said. "Not while Dame DeWitt is out there with a gun." He tossed her a flannel shirt. "Go back to the bedroom and change into that. Then you can sleep. I'll take the couch."

"I can take the couch," she protested.

"I," he said, "am going to sleep on the couch. Whether you're there or not."

She grinned and made a face at him, but retreated to the bedroom. When he went and tapped on the door later, carrying a cup of cocoa, she was sitting on the edge of the bed, staring at her reflection in the mirror. She looked small and rather lost in his big shirt which came down to her knees.

She took the warm mug between both hands, gulped thankfully at the hot liquid. "I just thought," she said, when she had finished. "What's the church going to do without money?"

He took the empty cup from her. "That's what insurance is for," he said, twitching back the blankets. "Stop worrying and go to bed."

She made another face, but obeyed, wiggling down under the blankets and pulling them up over her shoulder.

He touched the paint on her cheek, said in a gentler tone. "We'll manage. We have so far, haven't we?"

She smiled. "Yes. In our own blundering way. Enoch had better be proud of us!"

Back in the living room, Adam loaded his own revolver, snapped it shut, and laid it on a chair beside the couch. Grimm was exploring the room with a mincing step and disdainful sniffs. As he passed Shep, he showed the claws on one foot and hissed. Having put the other animal firmly in its place, he stalked grandly down the hallway towards the bedroom. Shep gave his master a reproachful look.

Leaning back on the couch with his hands behind his head, Adam said, "Better get used to it, old boy."

As the bridegroom rejoiceth
over the bride, so shall thy God
rejoice over thee.
Isaiah 62:5

Shaken awake, Genna peered groggily up at the one doing the shaking and made an incoherent grumble deep in her throat. She tried to turn away, pull the blankets over her head. A certain vague curiosity as to what Adam Cullen was doing in her bedroom didn't seem important enough to wake up over. It was probably just a dream anyway. So she was finally getting that kind of dream, was she? She smiled and prepared to sink back into warm oblivion.

The hand was insistent. Much too typically aggravating to be a dream Adam. "What?" she snarled in a tone muffled by the pillow.

"Time to get up," he said. "They haven't found Meredith yet, so you'll have to come down to the barn with me."

Her sleepy brain fumbled with that. Why should the lack of Meredith's presence mean she should have to help with chores? Meredith hadn't been doing it, had she? She giggled at the picture thus conjured of Meredith in overalls.

Adam got a good hold on the blankets and yanked, pitching them off the foot of the bed. This got an instantaneous reaction. Genna sat up with a shivering yelp. "Beast!" she said. "What are you doing here anyway?"

"I live here," he said. "Here's your clothes. A bit dirty but at least they're dry now. Get dressed, and I'll make some coffee."

"I don't drink coffee!" she yelled crossly after him. Smacked by the cold reality of a gray morning and goose-pimply legs, she felt events of the night before beginning to seep back into her consciousness like sludge. Crossing her arms tightly over her flannel-clad chest, she peered at the bedside clock for distraction. 5:30. Indignation warmed her. 5:30! The man must be mad. What had he done with those blankets?

The phone shrilled by her elbow, sending her pulse skidding into overdrive. She snatched it up without thinking. "Hello?"

A pause, then Ben Grover's cautious tones, "Uh, is Adam there?"

A click and Adam's voice. "I've got it, Genna. You get dressed, you hear?"

A tingling blush chased all the chill from her body. She replaced the receiver very quietly, crept into clothes stiff with dried mud, traversed the hallway with what offended dignity she could muster.

Adam was still on the phone and turned his head to give her a wicked grin. The kettle was squealing, and she whisked it off the burner.

"Okay. See you." Adam said. Anybody that cheerful at 5:30 should be shot.

He gulped a cup of coffee while standing up. "Sure you don't want any? No time for breakfast now."

Her only answer was a glower.

"Okay," he said, strapping a pistol around his waist. "Let's go."

"Right behind you, John Wayne," she said sweetly. "It's only gentlemanly for you to get shot first."

"You aren't at your best in the morning, are you?" he asked, opening the door on a white mist that curled around the bottom steps.

"You call this morning?" The boots he had given her were miles too big, and she nearly stumbled over her own feet going down the steps. "To civilized people, this is the middle of the night."

Shuffling disconsolately along at his side, she crossed

her arms tightly over a coat that was also too big. The fog muffled sound, made the world eerily quiet, damp, and cold. She muttered something. He bent his head. "What?"

She cleared her throat, said with a loud kind of defiance. "I asked if you explained things to Ben."

"Oh, sure." He palmed the barn door open, looked down at her with profound innocence. "Whether he believed me is, of course, debatable. But don't worry. I think he'll keep it to himself. Though the cops, of course, know too."

"Know what?!"

"Where you were last night. When I called Lansky this morning to get an update, he was frantic. It was quite touching. I believe his exact words were, 'You didn't let that wacko painter go running off on her own again, did you? If somebody else in this crazy case gets themselves killed, my job is up for grabs.'"

"Touching," Genna agreed, "and what did you tell him?"

Adam opened his eyes wide. "Why the truth, of course. That you were safely tucked up in my bed all night. He was quite reassured."

"Why didn't you just issue a bulletin?" Genna inquired silkily, stomping ahead into the main aisle as he switched on the lights.

"Have a seat somewhere," Adam said. "You won't need to help out today. One of Ben's sons is coming over."

"I wasn't planning to," she retorted, looking about her. One of the cows on the end had shoved its hay up against a corner of the manger area. Genna elbowed her way between that cow and the next, ducked under the stanchions, patted the hay into a nest, and sank down on it. A row of cow faces looked at her in surprise. "Good night," she said to them, and closed her eyes.

She was awakened by a nudging around her legs, opened her eyes to find herself covered by purring barn cats with a cow trying to yank hay out from under her. Out on the drive people were talking.

She sat up, dusted off cats and hay, and staggered out to have a look. Adam and a younger version of Ben Grover were leaning on a police car, talking to Sergeant Rhys and another officer. They all turned to stare at her; the two police officers tried to conceal amused smirks. Looking down at her rumpled muddy skirts, and over-sized coat and boots, she could see why. "And I used to be such a sophisticate too," she said coldly. "What news?"

"Meredith turned herself in a half hour ago," Adam said, "with her lawyer."

"Thank you, God," Genna breathed. "I am going home."

They watched her shuffle off down the lane. "Unusual woman," the other cop ventured finally.

A couple days later, Adam was finally able to start plowing. He began with the big field that stretched down past Genna's place and, on each pass, could see her working in her garden. The day was fair and seventyish, and fruit trees had erupted into hectic bloom to compete with the last of the daffodils and the first of the dandelions. He had deliberately chosen his older tractor, the one without a cab, so that he could feel the sunlight on his shoulders. Shep trotted along behind the tractor and made a big show of digging things out of the freshly turned soil and, when they passed Genna's, merrily chased her cat up a tree.

Grimm went along with this, spitting and arching dramatically, but he knew as well as Adam that Shep, for a farm dog, was strangely softhearted. He never killed any of the things he caught, was more likely, in fact, to lick them solicitously enough to drown them—which had not been much help in controlling the groundhog population.

The cat curled up comfortably on a warm limb and went to sleep. Apparently finding this an attractive idea, Shep plopped down underneath the tree to take a nap of his own. Then the only noise was the tractor's sputter and the chirping of birds attracted to worms and bugs in the fresh brown furrows.

So, both man and woman worked, in a kind of communion of satisfaction with the cool soil and the warm sun. On one of his turns back up the field, Adam saw Ben Grover waiting for him. He stopped the tractor at the end of the row and got off to talk. Grover had his granddaughter with him, and the little girl ran on down the lane to see Genna. The two men followed her desultorily as they talked, stopped to lean against the tree beside the garden. They had plenty to discuss. The search for a new pastor had to be started and wasn't going to be easy; there weren't enough pastors to go around these days. They agreed that Elliot Bentley might make it after all. His money was gone, his company would fold, the big house would have to be auctioned off. But he had agreed to undergo counseling. He was still staying with Ben, helping with the farming—what many of his compatriots might think a big step down, but the two men chatting under the tree didn't see it that way.

There was the possibility that he might be able to reunite with his family. But happy endings didn't happen overnight. The biggest obstacle they'd feared—Tanya's resistance to any such plan—had never materialized. "Yes," the girl had agreed. "She should get back with him if she can. She still loves him, you know, and I wouldn't want to leave her alone when I go to college. But only if he changes." *She* still loves him. Any affection on Tanya's part, it was implied, would be slow in returning. One couldn't blame her for that.

Genna and the little girl were having a tea party, making stiffly formal faces and giggling over their china cups. By the time the men strolled over to them, they had put the cups down on the large flat rock that served as a table and were making mud pies.

The child wailed when her grandfather said they should be going. "But we're not done with the tea!"

"Oh, I'm sure Mr. Cullen will be happy to finish up yours for you," Grover said with a grin and a wink.

Playing along, Adam sat down across from Genna and picked up a cup, extending a little finger stiffly and speaking with an awful British accent. "Jolly good show, Miss Leon."

The granddaughter went into a fit of giggles and allowed herself to be led away.

Genna giggled too. She picked up her own cup with dirty fingers and offered one of the mud pies. "Do have a scone, Mr. Cullen. Cook is so proud of them."

Dressed in yards of flowered cotton, she looked young and fresh-faced and happier than he'd seen her in some time.

"No thank you, Miss Leon," Adam said with stiff formality. "Not quite my cup of tea, don'tchaknow."

Genna giggled harder and flung the mud pie at him. He dodged it easily and tut-tutted. "*Not* behavior becoming a lady."

She drank from her cup. Antique china. It was like her to use that for a mud pie party. Peering at him wickedly over the rim, she said, "I can't help noticing you and Ben are getting along better."

"Yes, you may now say, 'I told you so,'" Adam replied

agreeably. "We are both considering changing our methods, actually, and going the organic route. That's what I wanted to ask his advice about before. And I was sure surprised to hear that he'd been considering it too."

Pink-cheeked with suppressed excitement, Genna breathed, "You're going organic? For that, I'll forgive you anything!"

"Anything?" Something in his speculative gaze discomfited her and she looked away, flushing.

"Of course, it'll be risky," he said, "and it'll take years to make the transition properly. I never would have even considered it before, but now . . ."

"But now—" she prodded.

"There are other things that seem more important than security." He was still looking at her, and flustered, she took a large gulp of tea. "I think I'm in love with you," he finished in the same calm, matter-of-fact tone. "Would you consider marrying me?"

She choked on the tea, spluttered, and almost dropped her cup. "What?" she gasped finally.

"You heard me."

She was tense, wary, like a startled animal. But she conjured up a weak smile from somewhere. "It hardly seems likely. I'm not your type."

He eyed her critically. "No, you're sloppy, you're childish, you're impulsive, and right now you have a big streak of mud across your nose." Her smile was going resentfully stiff. "All of which," he concluded, "might explain my almost overwhelming impulse to kiss you."

Red-faced, she hissed, "Well, I certainly don't want to kiss you!"

"Why not? What's a kiss after all?"

She read a certain challenge in that. What's so important about one little kiss?

She chewed on her lip, staring blindly down at her cup as she tried to think this through.

"All right," she said finally, flatly, putting the cup down on the rock. "You can kiss me if that will show you how crazy this all is. But don't expect to enjoy it. I am not good at this lovey-dovey stuff." She edged gracelessly around the rock on her knees, mud-encrusted hands held out away from herself to avoid getting her dress or his shirt dirty, tilted her head up and squinched her eyes shut, wearing the expression of a martyr. "All right. Kiss me."

Having deduced correctly that he was not much more experienced at this kind of thing than she was, she expected a mild peck. Instead he put a hand at her back and yanked. She overbalanced and fell against him with a startled yelp, clutching with both hands and opening her eyes to glare surprise. His face was very close to hers. What she saw in it for the briefest of instants before she shut her eyes against that knowledge convinced her that he wasn't kidding.

She did not hear rockets, see fireworks, or feel the

earth move. What she did feel was a man's strong arms and the warmth of spring light on her face before he blocked it out and kissed her and the thundering of a pulse so heavy that she wondered if she were feeling his heartbeat as well as her own. She panicked as she felt him start to let her go, pushed closer under the compulsion of a restless, resistless urging, opened her clenched hands and held on to his shoulders, opened her eyes and looked at him. She must have seemed frightened for he touched her face with that slow unhurried sureness of his that calmed jittery animals. Only not so sure this time; those rough, calloused fingers were far from steady. Even so, his eyes were mesmerizing.

She shook her head, jerked away, sat back on her heels and crossed her arms. "One of us has got to be sensible," she said. "It would never work. You know that." Her voice was almost pleading.

"Why not?"

She studied that with suspicion. The last 'why not?' had been more tricky than it seemed. This one she could answer.

"We don't even get along. It would be stupid. It would be—" She hesitated.

"Taking a dangerous chance?" he suggested. "What other way is there? Enoch taught us that. You go for all and risk everything, or you go for nothing and die safe. You look like the most reckless of us all, but I can see what Enoch meant when he said you and I were too much alike, both too careful. Let's try it the other way a while, shall we?"

Her face was strained with indecision. "I don't know if I love you," she said. "I hardly know what love means anymore."

"We'll have fun finding out then, won't we?" he said. He grinned. "I won't promise you peace, but I can guarantee you won't be bored." She looked wistful, shivered.

"But I don't go halfway on anything," he added, "and neither do you. If you say yes, there's no backing out if the going gets rough. So, are you done being sensible yet?"

The beginnings of a smile tugged her lips. "Well," she said tentatively, "sensible is something I never was very good at." The smile widened, tears of suppressed mirth glittered in her eyes. "And Uncle Leon only said I shouldn't sell you anything. I guess that rules out marrying you for your money."

He waited, as all love waits, smiling at the outrageousness of its own demands, promising only forever and asking everything. And in making this choice, she was making another also, or perhaps it was all one.

She went up on her knees again. "Yes!" she said, and threw herself into his arms. And, somehow, they were both laughing.

Lansky and Rhys drove through Deerfield again on their way to someplace else. On impulse, Rhys stopped the car; they both got out and stood looking at the church. An elderly sedan raced recklessly in reverse out of the parsonage driveway, ground to a halt in the middle of the road upon its occupants noticing the police officers. "Hal-lo!" Genna Leon cried.

The two men walked across to her. Ellen Foster smiled at them from the passenger seat. "Genna's going to teach me how to drive," she said.

Rhys made an involuntary noise that sounded like, "God!"

Genna regarded him suspiciously. "I didn't know that you were a praying man, Sergeant," she said sweetly. "We're going to town to look at wedding dresses. Then I'm going to buy some material so I can design one of my own."

Rhys made a half-gasp, half-cough that Genna chose to ignore.

"Then we're going to have a greasy cholesterol-ridden lunch, and go to see Meredith."

Lansky blinked. "I guess I should have expected that," he said. "Doesn't it bother you that the woman killed this guy you all adored over a couple thousand dollars?"

Genna squinted her eyes and looked away down the road. "I think it was one of Stevenson's characters who said that all sin is murder, and all life is war." She turned back to him. "Don't get me wrong. It wouldn't be love for me to excuse away what she did. God doesn't excuse sin; He forgives it. But we still have to bear its consequences. Enoch would have wanted us to help her bear them. He would know what it's like, having been in prison himself, you know."

"What?" Lansky gripped the car door. "Foster had a criminal record? And nobody ever mentioned that?"

"We didn't?" Genna shrugged. "Well, I guess it just wasn't relevant anymore, Lieutenant. It was when he was quite young, before he converted. I guess we just didn't think of it. But you see, don't you, why we have to go to Meredith? There's always a chance. She'll think we're fools, of course, but then," Genna's eyes twinkled, "she hasn't got the joke yet. That all of us are fools. We'll see you two. I'll send you invitations to the wedding." And the car shot away with a roar and a rattle.

"Was that a promise or a threat?" Lansky asked his sergeant as they walked back to their car.

He stopped to look again at the church, pointing its steeple up into a clear sky. "Tanya and her mother want to come back here for services. My wife says we should come with them."

"Careful, Lieutenant," Rhys cautioned. He gestured to a figure standing in the shadow of the building, staring up with tortured eyes at a stained glass window. Max Rourke. Seeing them, the writer turned, walked away very fast as if pursued by their stares. "Take a lesson from that one. They'll get you, if you aren't careful."

Lansky smiled strangely as he slid into the passenger's seat. "Is that," he asked, "a threat or a promise?"

About the Author

Audrey Stallsmith is a writer/artist who likes herbs and heirloom flowers, shaggy dogs, and old lace. She lives on a farm in western Pennsylvania.